The Black Stallion Revolts

The Black Stallion suddenly broke out of his paddock, hurled forth a screaming challenge and attacked Satan, in an adjoining paddock.

Henry Dailey, the trainer, told Alec Ramsay, "The Black's attack on Satan was the premeditated scheme of a murderer. Get smart, Alec, before he kills us all!"

Alec realized that the once wild stallion was restless from months of routine, so he took him on a plane bound for the West. There he would have acres and acres to roam. Little did Alec know that they were never to reach their destination, and that they would go separate ways before finding each other again.

Books by
WALTER FARLEY

The Black Stallion
The Black Stallion Returns
Son of the Black Stallion
The Island Stallion
The Black Stallion and Satan
The Black Stallion's Blood Bay Colt
The Island Stallion's Fury
The Black Stallion's Filly
The Black Stallion Revolts
The Black Stallion's Sulky Colt
The Island Stallion Races
The Black Stallion's Courage
The Black Stallion Mystery
The Black Stallion and Flame
The Black Stallion Challenged!
The Black Stallion's Ghost
The Black Stallion and the Girl
The Horse-Tamer
Man o' War

*All titles available in both paperback
and hardcover editions*

The Black Stallion Revolts

By WALTER FARLEY

Random House New York

Library of Congress Cataloging in Publication Data

Farley, Walter
  The black stallion revolts.
  New York, Random House [1953]
  I. Title.   PZ10.3.F22Bmb   53–6284‡
  Library of Congress [67y2]
  ISBN: 0–394–80609–3 (trade hardcover)
          0–394–90609–8 (library binding)
          0–394–83613–8 (trade paperback)

For Alice Patricia

Contents

The Sentinel

1

The gray gelding, Napoleon, was built from the ground up and butter fat. His roundness was not due to overfeeding or lack of exercise but to a most placid disposition and an ease of adapting himself to any kind of situation or way of life. He stood with one hind foot drawn in an easy, relaxed position and eyes half-closed. Only his long ears moved, and they just wobbled as if the weight of them was too much for him to bear at this particular moment. He was the picture of contentment; as peaceful as the June night which enveloped him. There was no reason for him to appear otherwise. He was most happy with his life. He was no youngster.

The grass of his paddock moved in the night breeze, giving it the soft, liquid motion of the sea. There were stars and a moon, and together they shone frostlike on the fences and roofs of the barns and main house a short distance away.

Finally the old gray roused himself to saunter about his paddock. His movements were slow and quiet. He was very particular in his choice of grass. He would stop only long enough to crop a few mouthfuls, then go on to other grasses that appealed more to his fancy and discriminating taste. But it wasn't long before he returned to his favorite haunt beneath the billowing oak tree. He closed his eyes again.

All was quiet, and as it should be. The inky silhouette of a tall, black stallion moved in the adjacent paddock to his left. Teeth clicked sharply as the stallion cut the grass low and even.

The gray's wobbling ears were keen, and by using them he followed the movements of the Black. He was well aware, too, of the whereabouts of the burly, black horse in still another paddock, the one on his right. He had heard Satan snort a few moments ago.

The breeze became stronger, gently whipping his body with a shower of deep evening coolness. After the heat of day it felt very good. That there were no flies to bother him added to his enjoyment. For ideal comfort this was the way it should be. A fly-protected barn during the day, and at night the freedom of the paddocks. For several weeks now the horses had been allowed this privilege. It would continue as long as there was peace in the paddocks. All this the old gray knew very well; his vast experience told him so.

He knew why he occupied the paddock between the

Black and Satan. To keep his head, to think for himself, to do what was expected of him . . . these things he had learned long ago. He did his duties willingly, whether he was on the track, helping to school young and eager yearlings in their first lessons, or here in the paddock, where he was ever watchful of the actions of mature stallions. Knowing that he was wanted, that he had a job to do, gave him a warm consciousness of virtue and well-being. He opened his eyes, took in the paddock fences, and then, as though receiving comfort and security from their great height, permitted his eyelids to drop again. This time he went fast asleep.

He awakened to the sound of a strong wind. The skies had turned black. The moon was blanketed by heavy, running clouds and the stars were mere pinpoints in the heavens, shedding no light below. The oak tree afforded the gray horse protection against the wind and he was loath to leave it. Besides, there was no reason for him to go. He need only stay here and wait out the wind. If it got worse and became a storm, he was certain that soon he would see the lights go on in the house and barn, and shortly thereafter he and the others would be taken into their stalls. He moved closer to the great trunk of the tree, and for a while just listened to the racing winds above him.

It was the wind and the blackness of the night that diverted Napoleon's attention from the movements of the tall stallion in the next paddock. For a long while the Black had trotted lightly and warily along the fence, only his eyes disclosing the excitement that burned within him. He made no sound except for the slight, hushed beat of his hoofs over the grass. He did not shrill his challenge to the burly stallion two paddocks away from him. It was not yet time. The Black was clever and able to control the savage instinct that sought release within his great body.

The wind whipped his mane, and his tail, set high, billowed behind him. He stopped again to measure the height of the fence. In spite of his long limbs he had to stretch his head to touch the top board. He moved on to the front corner of the paddock, facing the barn. Once more he tested his strength against the center boards at this particular spot. They bent as they had before. He pushed harder this time. They cracked and split. He stopped using his strength, waiting almost cunningly until deciding on his next move. The fire in his eyes was mounting.

Carefully he lowered himself to the ground, pressing the weight of his body against the bottom board. Then he rolled away and struck a smashing blow against it with his hind feet. It split as had the others. Still on his back, he rolled back and forth, using his great body like a pendulum against the boards. But he did not ram his weight like a blundering bruiser. Instead, with cunning and skill he maneuvered his body, using pressure against the split boards only when he knew they were most apt to give completely. Finally they broke and were swept outward as he rolled under the top board. The Black was free of his confining paddock!

He got to his feet with the speed and agility of the wildest and most savage of animals. A striking change had swept over his glistening body. No longer was he calm and cunning, but trembling and brutally eager *to kill.* Gone was his domesticity and the inner control that had kept the fire from his eyes and given the coolness to his blood. Now he was inflamed with a terrible but natural instinct to do battle with another stallion. He turned his gleaming, red eyes on Satan, two paddocks beyond; then he hurled forth his screaming challenge, and its shrillness rose above the cry of the wind.

He was already on his way down the dirt road fronting the paddocks when the gray gelding came plunging to the fence. The stallion paid not the slightest attention to him. The gray ran with his ears back, his teeth snapping in rage between the boards because he knew the stallion's savage intent, and could do nothing to keep him from the black horse beyond. The gelding stopped when he came to the end of his enclosure. He neighed loudly and incessantly, knowing this was the only useful thing he could do. But his warnings of the disturbed peace were deadened by the force of the wind. The house and barn remained dark.

Turning from the dirt road, the tall stallion ran down the corridor between the paddocks. Every possible pre-caution had been taken to make the paddocks foolproof, to keep one stallion from another, to forestall just such an emergency as this. The paddock fences were strong and high, the corridor wide. Yet the Black was loose, and in spite of the fence still separating him from Satan, his fury was not to be denied. He ran with reckless speed down the corridor and back again, once hurling himself against the fence only to be repelled. He ignored the gray gelding, who followed his every move still neighing in rage. He had eyes only for the large, black horse who stood so quietly in the center of his paddock. That Satan did not move, that he uttered no scream accepting the challenge, infuriated the tall stallion even more. His nostrils were distended in recognition of the hateful scent of his rival as he finally left the corridor and approached Satan's paddock from the front.

He went to the fence screaming. Lifting his head, he touched his nose to the top board. Then he rose on hind legs to bring his forehoofs down upon it. He was terrible in his fury, but his act proved futile. Frenzied rage had replaced the cool cunningness of his earlier behavior. He rose again, trying to batter down the fence, and his legs hurt from the crashing impact of his blows. The fence remained intact. He whirled while still at his utmost height, his hind legs pivoting his great body with uncanny grace and swiftness, then sending him away from the fence in long strides. It was less than a hundred feet to the barn, and there he stopped short with tossing head and mane. With no hesitation he whirled again and swept back, his strides lengthening with startling swiftness for so short a distance. He gathered his great body in front of the fence as though to jump it, but he never unleashed his spring. Instead he stopped short again, stomping the earth with both forefeet in his frenzy and frustration.

He turned to the left to run along the fence. He had passed the paddock gate when suddenly he felt the earth rise gradually beneath his running hoofs, and then descend abruptly. He went on for a short distance before stopping and going back to the elevated stretch of ground which was used in the loading and unloading of horses from vans. Now he was more quiet, more cunning. He walked up the gradual ascent to the flat summit of the grassy mound. For a moment he stood there, his wild eyes seeming to measure the distance to the fence. His added height enabled him to see over the top board, and he screamed again at the horse beyond. There was a new note to his whistle, for now he knew the battle was close at hand. Satan, too, was aware of it; he screamed for the first time . . . and his answer was as shrill, as terrible in its savageness as his challenger's.

The Black turned, leaving the mound, and went once more as far as the barn. He whirled and bolted, picking up speed with every stride. He gathered himself going up the grassy incline. At the top he rose in the air, hurling himself forward, his legs tucked well beneath him. A hoof struck the top of the fence but did not upset him. He came down and, without breaking stride, raced forward to meet Satan.

He went only a short distance before he came to a plunging stop, the cool logic that had helped him win battles with other stallions coming to the fore. His eyes were still blazing with hate, his ears were flat against his head. But when he moved again it was to encircle his opponent with strides that were light and cautious.

Both fear and fire shone in Satan's eyes. He did not want to fight yet he stood unflinching and ready. He was heavier than the Black, though not as tall. His bones were larger, his neck shorter and more bulging with muscle, his head heavier. Yet his great, thick body had the same fascination and swiftness of movement as the stallion who encircled him. He had inherited these together with his tremendous speed from the Black, his sire. Now, keeping his bright eyes on his opponent, Satan began to move with him. He heard him scream again, and answered. He waited for the fight to be brought to him. He was ready.

Yet when the attack came, it was with the swiftness of light, and even though Satan had thought himself prepared he barely had time to rise and meet the horrible onslaught. Two raging furies, hateful to see, began a combat that would end only with the death of one!

The first light that went on was in the apartment over the broodmare barn, just past the main house. Seconds later a short, stocky man, wearing only pajamas and slippers, came running out the door. He moved ghostlike in the wind, his face as white as his disheveled hair. His bowlegs spun like a wheel as his strides came faster. He lost one loose slipper. He kicked the other off without breaking his run. Only when he came to the main house did he stop, and then just for a second. Cupping large hands around his mouth, he let loose a scream in the direction of the open window on the second floor.

"Alec! Alec! Alec!"

The wind hurled his cries aside. He didn't know if he'd been heard and he couldn't wait to find out. He started running again, his blood hammering within his chest, but not from his exertion. His eyes were dimmed and wet, but not from the wind. He had just seen the Black clear the fence into Satan's paddock. He knew what the consequences would be.

Nearing the fence, he saw the silhouette of the attacker encircling Satan. He knew he was too late, that the clash of bodies would come in seconds. His face grew even paler, yet uncontrollable rage was there, too. His body and voice trembled as he roared, *"Away! Away, you killer!"* But he knew the Black didn't hear him, and that even if he did the command would have little effect.

He ran to the stallion barn and flung open the door, looking for any weapons he might use. A leather riding whip hung on a peg in the entryway. He took it. A pitchfork stood by the door. He grabbed this, too, and ran outside again. Reaching the paddock gate, he pulled it open wide, and charged toward the black bodies now wrapped in a deadly embrace.

He screamed at them, but his voice was just a muted whisper beneath the crashing blows of forehoofs that pounded in furious battle. Suddenly, from their great height, the stallions toppled and fell, their bodies shaking the very earth. The man sprang forward, trying to get between them with his pitchfork. But their action was too fast and terrifying, and his efforts were futile. They bounded to lightning feet and clashed again, their heads extended long and snakelike as they sought with bared teeth to tear and rend each other.

Unmindful of his own safety, the man moved forward with his puny weapons. As yet neither stallion had drawn blood. But in a matter of seconds, if he couldn't separate them, it would be too late. They were locked together, seemingly suspended in the air. Each sought the other's windpipe for the vicious hold that would mean certain death. The man's breath came in fast, hard gasps as he tried to thrust the pitchfork between them, to divert their attention to him. Even now he knew he could control Satan if he ever got the chance. But there would be no opportunity, not with the Black, *that hellion,* forcing the fight, determined on destruction!

The stallions lost their holds, and came screaming down again. The Black whirled, letting fly his hind hoofs in an awful blow which, if it had landed full, would have sent Satan reeling. But the burly horse saw the hoofs coming. He shifted his great body with amazing agility, and the crashing hind legs only grazed him. Nevertheless, although he had avoided serious injury, the glancing blow sent him off balance. He stumbled and went down.

At this moment the man plunged forward, reaching the Black before he could whirl on the fallen horse. In his fury he used the leather riding crop, bringing it down hard again and again against the stallion's lathered hindquarters. A great tremor racked the Black's body as the blows landed. Suddenly he turned upon the man, all his savageness now directed upon him.

With pitchfork extended the man fell back. He shouted futile commands as the stallion plunged toward him and then stopped before the steel prongs of the fork. The man knew his life was in great danger, yet he stole a second to glance at Satan, who was climbing to his feet. If only Satan would go through the open gate of the paddock! If only he could keep the Black away and get out himself!

He backed toward the gate shouting, *"Out, Satan! Out!"* But the words barely left his lips before the Black came at him again, and he raised the pitchfork in his defense. He struck hard, viciously, and the stallion fell back.

The man saw Satan moving toward the gate. Then he saw Alec, running past the horse. He shouted the boy's name and waited for him, without lowering his pitchfork.

Alec came to a stop. He stood still until he was certain the Black's wild eyes were on him, then he walked forward, his bare feet making no sound.

Still pale with rage and terror, the man cried, "Take the whip, Alec! Use it on him if you have to!"

Without taking his eyes off the Black, Alec said, "If I did, he'd kill me, Henry. The same as he would have killed you." He continued walking forward, talking to the stallion in a soft, low voice, and never raising it or his hand in a gesture of any kind. Only once did he interrupt his murmurings with a soft-spoken command. When he got close to the Black, he put his hand on the lathered halter. The stallion trembled, and for a moment his eyes gleamed brighter than ever. Alec gave the low command again, but the stallion drew back his head in an abrupt gesture of defiance.

Keeping his hand on the halter, Alec moved along with the stallion until he came to a stop. The boy waited patiently, his eyes never leaving those of his horse, his murmurings never ceasing. With a motion of his head, he indicated to Henry that he was to leave.

Alec turned the Black toward the upper end of the paddock, diverting his attention from Satan and Henry.

With his free hand he tried to soothe the tossing head, and finally he got the stallion to take a few steps up the paddock. Then the Black stopped again, trying to turn his head.

Alec held him close, and waited for a while before leading him forward once more. Satan and Henry had left the paddock. It was a little easier now. The Black followed Alec for a moment before stopping again, this time to utter his short, piercing blast. Alec stood quietly beside him, the wind billowing his pajamas. He knew that in a little while the Black would calm down, and he would be able to take him into the barn. But right now he must go on as he was doing, talking to him, soothing him, and waiting.

He walked him again, and as he did, he tried to understand the reason for the Black's sudden, vicious attack on Satan. For many months his horse had been all a well-mannered stallion should be. Why, then, had he reverted to the role of a killer tonight? And what were he and Henry going to do about it?

Revolt!

2

Alec stood outside the heavy oak door of the Black's stall. He heard him rustling his straw, and through the iron-barred window watched him move restlessly about. The fierce light had left the stallion's eyes, and Alec knew that in a few minutes it would seem as if he had never shown rage, as if his fury had never been aroused. Yet within him that savage, natural instinct to kill would live, smoldering and waiting for some spark to set it aflame again. It would never die.

Alec turned from the Black to watch Henry in his never-ending walk up and down the long corridor, his voice still raised in furious tirade against the stallion. As with the Black, it would take a little while for Henry to quiet down, thought Alec. He'd be able to talk to him sensibly then. But not now. Now he could only listen, and wait.

Henry came down the corridor. "He would have killed Satan! In another minute he'd have done it!" He turned on his heel quickly with only a glance at Alec. Again he walked up the corridor, his bare grass-stained feet making no sound. "He would have killed me, too! Just like that!" He snapped his large, rugged fingers.

Henry passed Napoleon's stall. The old gray had his large head down as though he were assuming all blame for the night attack and thought that Henry's loud denunciation was meant for him alone. Satan was in a stall at the far end of the barn, and only there did Henry come to a stop, to speak softly. There was no doubt of his love for Satan. It was in his eyes and voice for anyone to see. He had raised Satan from a colt. He had trained him carefully and wisely, making him a perfect racing machine, a great champion.

Alec waited, never moving from the Black's door while Henry resumed his pacing. The overhead lights were harsh and cruel to his old friend. They emphasized the deep lines in Henry's face and his dropped jowls. They made his disheveled hair look whiter and thinner.

A few more trips up and down the corridor, and then Henry's pace slowed. There were longer lapses between his sentences. Alec knew that it wouldn't be long now before they'd be able to discuss intelligently the Black's vicious attack on Satan, the reasons for it, and the precautionary measures that must be taken to prevent its happening again. Finally, Henry came to a stop before him.

"You've said nothing, Alec, nothing at all! Don't you

realize what he did? What could have happened to Satan?''

"And to *you*," Alec added. "Yes, I know, Henry."

Henry's jaw came out, his unshaven face bristling with stiff, gray hair. "Then why do you take it so calmly, just as though you didn't care?"

"I do care. I'm not calm. But shouting's not going to help us work it out."

"It helps *me!*" Henry bellowed. He turned fiercely and went up and down the corridor again. When he came back he said bitterly, "Okay, Alec, let's have it your way, then. You want to sit down nice-like and talk it all over quietly as if we're just havin' a little trouble with an unruly yearling." His jaw quivered while he paused for breath. When he spoke again, all his anger and fury had returned. "Get smart, Alec! This is no yearling we're dealin' with. Get smart before he kills all of us!"

Alec's mouth tightened, and white showed at his cheek bones. He kept quiet. He had to understand Henry, just as he did the Black. He had to remember never to force an issue with either of them. Trying to push them around, battling their wills, would get him nowhere. Ask them nicely and he had a chance.

Henry had turned to the Black's window, and was watching the tall stallion. "It's not as if this fight was something that just flared up in a moment," the trainer said. "This took time, a lot of time, a lot of planning. It took cunning to break down the fence, and then find a way into Satan's paddock. His attack was no sudden, natural urge to fight another stallion, but the methodical, vicious, premeditated scheme of a *murderer*!''

For a moment the barn was quiet and they could hear the wind blowing outside.

Alec said, "Where'd we get the Black, Henry?"

The trainer's small, boring eyes left the stallion. "You're being silly. What do you mean where'd we get him?"

"Just that, Henry. We got him in Arabia. He was foaled and raised in the Great Desert, the Rub' al Khali."

"I know all that."

"I thought maybe you'd forgotten," Alec said.

"Forgotten?" Henry sought an explanation in Alec's eyes. "Forgotten that he was desert born? What do you take me for, Alec?" He raised his voice a pitch higher. "Do you think that excuses him for *this*? Wasn't Satan desert born, too?"

"Satan came to us as a weanling," Alec said quietly. "He had a chance. The Black was a mature stallion, never fully broken, never handled. And, Henry, he had roamed the desert *free* for a long while. Have you forgotten that?"

"I tell you I haven't forgotten anything," the old man said. Some of the harshness was gone from his voice. "I know further that he's your horse completely, that no other person in this world can do as much with him. But Alec . . ."

"Do you remember my telling you what happened the first time I ever saw him," Alec interrupted, "the day they were loading him on board my ship when it stopped at that Arabian port on the Red Sea?"

Henry shook his head in disgust. "Alec, if you're going to bother tellin' me the whole story of the Black again, you'd better just save your breath an' I'll save you some time. I know he was stolen from the Arab sheikh Abu Ishak, and put aboard your ship. I know it went down off the west coast of Spain and you and the Black were the only survivors. An' if he hadn't pulled you to that reef of an island somewhere out there you wouldn't be around now to be talkin' this way." Henry paused for breath. "I know, too, that if you hadn't found food for him on the island, he wouldn't be any more yours than he's mine or anyone else's. A hungry animal is a tame animal. I've seen it happen before. Sure, I'll admit he loves you now, but never forget that your finding something for him to eat when he was starving made it all possible."

"I wasn't going into all that." Alec said.

"You brought it up," Henry insisted, his mouth less tight now. "I'll finish it. I don't want you to think I've forgotten *anything*," he added sarcastically. "When you came back to the States with him, I met you and him for the first time. I knew what kind of a horse you had better'n you did. We raced him once and there never was or will be another race like it. Then we lost him because his rightful owner, Abu Ishak, came to reclaim him. Later on he sent you Satan as your reward, and then when Abu died he willed you the Black, so we got him back again."

Henry stopped. "Am I making sense, Alec? Isn't my memory still good?"

Alec nodded, and tried to interrupt. "All I wanted to say, Henry, was . . ."

"Let me finish, Alec. So we had the Black and Satan, and we made a world champion of Satan. It enabled us to set up this place." Henry's hands went out in a great gesture. "We have one of the country's finest stock farms and racing stables. Sure, Alec, we've arrived in the big time, and we're more than payin' our way along. An' we owe it all to the Black and Satan. Without them you and I would be back in the suburbs of New York City. You ridin' subways instead of horses, and I sittin' in a chair tryin' to remember the old days when I was a lot younger and had a way with horses. Sure and I'd be grievin' about it being all over."

Henry paused for a moment, his yellowing teeth biting into his lower lip. Then he went on. "But what has all that got to do with what happened tonight, Alec? How does all this business of remembering what's happened before, and appreciating what we have now, got to do with the viciousness, the ruthlessness of what *he* did tonight?"

"It helps us to understand him and the reasons for his attack on Satan."

"But I do understand," Henry came back, emphasizing every word, every letter. "That's what I've been telling you."

"You do now, but you didn't. Not a few minutes ago," Alec said. "You didn't give yourself a chance."

"So I blew off steam," Henry said.

"So you did," Alec agreed. "And now you're all quieted down."

"All quieted down," Henry repeated. "If we're goin'

to talk any more let's go into the office. Let the horses get some quiet too.''

They left the corridor, turning off the light behind them, and entered the barn's office. As Henry sat down in the deep cushioned chair behind the desk, Alec straddled a straight chair before it.

''You still haven't let me say what I wanted to,'' Alec said. ''About what happened the time I first saw the Black.''

''He was a terror on the pier,'' Henry recalled.

''More than that. He killed a man,'' Alec returned quietly.

Henry's face became taut. ''Yes, I remember you told me that.''

''I told you why he did it, too, didn't I?''

Henry nodded. ''Someone used a whip on him.''

''That's right,'' Alec said. ''And you used one on him tonight. That's why he turned on you.''

''But what was I going to do, Alec? He was about to kill Satan!''

''I know, but the point is you forgot. He would have taken anything else from you but a whip. You've never had any trouble with him before.''

''All right, I forgot,'' Henry said brusquely. ''But where do we go from here? What are we going to do about him?''

''Nothing. There's nothing we *can* do except always keep his background in mind, and never forget it. I think we've both been inclined lately to do just that.''

''He's given us every reason to forget what he was,''

Henry insisted. "He's been easy to handle, and a good-mannered stallion. At times he's been just as nice as Satan. He's taken to stable routine like a park hack."

"That's just it," Alec said. "He's been good too long. The break had to come sometime, and it came tonight. Unfortunately, neither of us was figuring on such a thing happening. We're as much to blame."

Henry left his chair to walk nervously about the room. His eyes swept over the walls, taking in the numerous championship plaques that had been awarded to Satan during his racing career. "Do you think he's gotten it out of his system for a while then?" he asked.

"I don't know, Henry. Maybe. Maybe not. I don't think there's any way of telling for sure."

"Then the only thing we can do is to isolate him until we find out," the trainer said. "Put him in one of the far pastures or keep him in the barn most of the time."

"Isolation might make things worse," Alec said quietly.

"I know, but we can't take any chances of him gettin' to Satan again."

Alec's gaze left Henry and shifted to the east window. The horizon was turning a dull gray. Soon the day would begin. There was no sense in going back to bed now. In a little while it would be time to feed the broodmares and their colts, to handle the weanlings and yearlings, to do the many other endless tasks that went with the operation of a stock farm. Routine and schedules. Regular hours for feeding, handling, cleaning and training. But in spite of all this his days were never dull. Every colt and filly, every broodmare and stallion was an individual to be treated in his or her own special way to obtain best results. Yet there were only so many hours in a day with so many jobs to be done. Keep to a schedule and one finished in time for bed.

Hearing the Black neigh jolted Alec's mind back to the problem at hand. If the stallion was a person, one would say he was tired of routine, tired of the regularity of his daily schedule. All right, Alec thought, say it. . . . *He's bored!* Say it and get it over with! Not so long ago the Black had roamed the Great Desert of Arabia, wild and free. Now he was being treated like the most domesticated of farm animals. Was it any wonder that he had revolted against it all? Wasn't it, indeed, a wonder that he hadn't revolted long before tonight? The Black needed freedom, a freedom he couldn't have here no matter what arrangements were made!

"Henry . . ."

"Yeah?"

"What do you do when you get pretty fed up with farm routine?" Alec asked.

Henry looked puzzled. He walked around to the front of the desk and then sat down again, hoping to meet Alec's gaze. But the boy's eyes were fixed on the desk.

"You can't say I get fed up," Henry said. "I like it here. I just need a change every once in a while."

"So you take one or more of our horses to the track for a season's campaign."

"Sure, Alec. That's part of my job here. Racing helps to pay our bills." Henry grinned sheepishly. "But what are you driving at?"

"The point I'm trying to make is that you'd be a pretty

unruly guy if you couldn't get back to the track once in a while."

"Naturally. It's been an important part of my life for some fifty years. It's *me*."

"It's the Black too," Alec said quietly.

"Racing?" Henry asked incredulously. "Are you out of your mind, Alec? He's not controllable on a track. You know that as well as I do."

"I didn't mean racing," Alec said quickly. "But just as training and racing are important to you, freedom is necessary to the Black."

Henry laughed. "Sure," he said, "but what do you want to do? Turn him loose to roam wherever he pleases?"

"That's exactly what I mean."

"You're kidding." But the smile left Henry's lips when he met Alec's gaze. "Can't you just see him running around the countryside? Maybe he'll even head down the Parkway to New York City for a look at the race tracks."

"Now you're trying to be funny," Alec said.

"Okay, I was tryin'," Henry returned gravely. "But you suggested this, so let's hear you come up with some kind of an explanation."

"He needs a change from the routine and daily schedule he's had here at the farm. He's behaved himself for a long, long while but tonight was the turning point. We won't have a moment's peace around here from now on. I'm convinced of that, now that I've thought it all over. Give him some freedom, a chance to roam and be on his own again, and it'll get a lot of out of his system. He'll come back a better horse for it."

"Come back? Come back from where?"

"How about Bill Gallon's place in southern California?"

"The Desert Ranch? You mean, Alec, you want to send him 'way out there? Why?"

"Because Bill Gallon has several thousand fenced acres of desert and irrigated pastureland," Alec said quietly. "The Black would have something like his homeland. He'd have freedom to roam. It's the closest thing I can think of to what he needs right now. Do you think Bill would let us turn him out there for a month, maybe two months?"

"Of course. He's one of my best friends, isn't he? But, Alec . . ." Henry paused. "You really think that'll do the trick? You just want him turned loose?"

"That's all," Alec said. "It'll be enough."

"You should go with him. He's your horse."

Alec's gaze dropped to the huge desk in front of him. "I'll take him out there, anyway."

"And then come back?" Henry asked.

"Yes, just as soon as I know everything is all right."

"Why don't you stay with him?"

"You know why, Henry."

"Your work here?"

Alec nodded.

Henry was quiet for a few minutes, but his eyes never left Alec's face. Finally he said, "Maybe you need a change, too."

"No, I'm fine."

"But you'll miss him."

"Sure."

"And he'll miss you."

"He'll be too happy, too free to miss anybody," Alec said.

"Having just you around would make his freedom all the more exciting," Henry said. "Just the two of you, like it was at first."

Alec smiled. "You're getting sentimental, Henry."

"Sure, but I'd like to see you go with him, if you're serious about all this."

"I'm serious, all right."

Henry stood up. "He's your horse, so you stay with him. I'll take over your jobs here, and with your dad and Jinx to help I'll have no trouble. In fact, it'll do me good to assume some responsibility around here for a change."

Alec rose from his chair. "No, Henry. I'll come back."

"So you think you're indispensable?"

"No, it isn't that."

"Sure it is, and that's a bad state of mind." Henry came around the desk, and took Alec by the arm. "If the Black goes, you go too . . . and you stay with him until he comes back. That's decided. Now let's get out of these pajamas."

As they left the office Alec asked, "Will you call Bill Gallon today to see if it's all right with him?"

"Sure. When do you want to leave?"

"As soon as we can charter a plane. The sooner the better, now that we've decided to get him out of here."

"Yeah, I guess so," Henry returned. "No sense puttin' it off, not after tonight."

After Henry had left, Alec stood for a few minutes in the darkened corridor. The air was heavy with the smells of oiled leather, and soap, and hay, and grain. All this had become so much a part of him. Wouldn't he worry about the mares and their foals, the yearling colts and fillies while he was away? He supposed so, but it was needless. There was competent help here and, as Henry had said, no person was indispensable.

He heard the Black nickering, and his heart pounded while he thought of the two of them being alone again. Remember the island? Remember his first ride on the Black? Remember Arabia? Remember riding the Black across the desert and the steady beat of the stallion's hoofs in the sand? Yes, in spite of his love for the farm, it would be good to be alone with his horse again. Like the Black, he wanted to be free for a while.

Without turning on the lights, he walked down the long corridor. He'd tell the great stallion what they were going to do, and somehow the Black would understand. Not from his words, but through some other way, which he himself didn't understand and could only accept.

Winged Fury

3

Two days later they stood within the close confines of a plane that had been specially equipped for the air transportation of horses. The floor of the horse pullman was lower than in passenger planes, providing additional head space, and the Black stood cross-tied in a boxed stall. He had given Alec no trouble while being loaded, following him up the ramp docilely and hesitating only before the rooftop doorway that had been raised high to give him more headroom upon entering the plane.

Now Alec adjusted the meshed-rope sling before the stall so his horse could more easily get at the hay it held. The Black pulled a mouthful from the sling, but held the hay between his lips without chewing, his large eyes wandering over the interior of the plane. He pawed for a while at the wood shavings beneath his hoofs, found the

28

rubber matting beneath, and then his gaze finally returned to Alec. He began chewing the hay.

Henry said, "Until they find a better way of securing a horse inside a plane, air-shipping isn't for me."

Alec watched the stallion shift his weight from one side of his close stall to the other, and then shake his head as much as his tie ropes would allow. "They secure them as well as possible," Alec said. "Give a horse no room to move at all, and you'll only have more trouble."

"I suppose so," Henry admitted. He paused. "Well, Alec, I guess this is it for a while." His smile belied the soberness he felt. "You two have a good vacation, and don't worry about the farm. We'll do all right. You give my best to Bill. Tell him I'll be out there one of these days."

"I will, Henry."

"And be careful."

The captain and copilot came up the ramp and into the plane. "We're ready whenever you are," the captain said.

Henry slapped Alec gently on the back. "Okay, kid, have a good trip."

Alec walked to the ramp with him. "We'll be out there and all settled down by morning," he said. "That's the beauty of flying."

"Yeah, but you keep your eye on him every minute."

"Sure, but he'll give me no trouble. He's been up before and knows what it's all about."

"I know," Henry said. He stopped at the doorway. "Feed him light. Don't overload his stomach up there.

It's no place for him to get sick. Keep the blanket on him. It's bound to be a little drafty. Keep him warm.''

"Yes, Henry.'' Alec pushed his friend onto the ramp. "If you don't get going, I'll start advising you on the care and feeding of the horses back at the farm.''

Henry grunted. "That's not necessary.''

"I know.'' Alec smiled.

Upon reaching the ground, Henry helped close the portable lightweight ramp and get it inside the plane. The captain went to his compartment, but the copilot stayed behind to shut the rooftop doorway.

Alec went to his horse. The plane's takeoff might bother the Black a little.

"You'll be all right?'' the copilot asked.

"Sure.''

The man's eyes were on the stallion. "I've always wanted to see the Black,'' he said. "I saw him beat Cyclone and Sun Raider in that big match race in Chicago some years ago. I'll never forget it.''

"Nor I,'' Alec said.

"You never raced him again after that one, did you?''

"No.''

The copilot left, closing the door of the compartment behind him. The plane's engines shattered the quiet, sputtered, then settled into a steady drone. A few moments later they were moving and the Black shifted his weight to keep his balance.

"Easy, boy,'' Alec said softly.

Suddenly the plane came to a stop again, its engines slowing to idling speed. The cabin door opened, and the copilot returned.

"Your friend is out there shouting his head off about some keys . . . keys to the van, I believe he said."

Alec's hand went to his pocket. He'd forgotten to give Henry the ignition keys. He remembered, too, that in his wallet he was carrying the registration licenses for the van and all the other farm vehicles. Henry might need them during his absence. Quickly he took all his money from the wallet and, putting the keys inside, handed the wallet to the copilot. "You can throw him this," he said. "And if he can hear you, tell him all the registration licenses are there too. He can send me my wallet later."

The copilot left, and a few minutes later the plane was once more moving out to the airport's runway. Through the small windows, Alec caught a glimpse of Henry waving at them. Fortunately, Henry had only a short drive back to the farm from the local airport. He'd be home in time to see that the horses were all taken care of for the night.

But I'm supposed to be forgetting all that, Alec thought. This is our vacation.

The plane stopped again at the head of the runway. Its engines idled, and then after a few minutes they were revved up high. The plane shook with thunderous vibrations. Snorting, the Black pulled hard on his tie ropes, and Alec's hand went to him. The boy began talking, to soothe the Black, and continued while the plane fled down the runway to become airborne.

Only soft vibrations were felt as they climbed. The engines, too, were more quiet. Alec pulled the sliding blankets up on the Black's neck, making his horse more comfortable. There was nothing to take him away from his horse now, no other job to be done except to care for the Black. It was truly as it had been at the beginning, and it would go on and on for many wonderful weeks. He thought of the times they would share together again, and told the Black of them, knowing the stallion understood everything he said. It was a language all their own. It didn't necessarily consist of words, for Alec relied mainly on touches and soft sounds and quick movements of the eyes.

Alec told the Black of long days of bright sunshine with endless miles before him, of great hills and mountains showing blue against a pale sky, and beyond all these the desert that would be so bare and clean beneath his feet. He spoke of the nights too, the network of millions and billions of delicate stars that would be his roof as he rested after hard, exciting days. He didn't mention the fences that would keep him within Bill Gallon's ranch. There was no need. With thousands of wild acres to roam it would be as though there were no fences. Yet for Alec it was a comfort to know they were there, that somewhere on the Desert Ranch he would always be able to find the Black.

The stallion had settled down, and was pulling at his hay. Alec left him to get a drink of ice water from the cooler at the far end of the plane. He came back to sit on the tack trunk, thinking of how Henry had insisted upon his taking it, and how needless its contents were. He would use no brushes and currycombs on the stallion, no saddle or bridle when he rode him, no blankets at night. He would use nothing to remind the Black of the domesticity that had been left behind. The great stallion would be turned completely free, and Alec decided that he would not force himself upon the Black. The stallion would be ridden only when he asked for it, and Alec would know the signs.

The Black whinnied, and thrust his tongue out. Alec pulled it, then let go. The Black withdrew his tongue. This was a game they played. It meant there was no need for alarm or uneasiness. The Black was happy . . . and so was Alec, incredibly happy. The hours sped by, with the plane losing its race against a fast-dropping sun.

They refueled west of Chicago, and when they took to the air again it was through the dark sky of night. Alec hadn't left the plane or the Black's side during their short stop. He had given him a little grain, a little water, nothing more.

Long hours and miles passed as their flight progressed ever westward. The tall stallion had his eyes closed. Alec went over to the bucket seat at the side of the stall. He put a blanket on the metal seat and sat down, trying to make himself comfortable. He closed his eyes, but couldn't sleep. So he thought again of the new life that would begin for him and the Black within a few more hours. Or really *had* begun! Their old life at the farm was already many hours behind them.

Here he was alone with his horse, the finest stallion in the world and still the fastest. Henry might not think so. Henry would say that there never had been a horse with more speed than Satan, never would be. And the racing world would probably agree with him. But with Satan retired from racing, the fans would forget him too, just as they had the Black. There were younger horses coming up each year to hold their attention. New track records were already being made. New champions were being crowned. Night Wind, owned by the High Crest Ranch in Texas, had been named "Horse-of-the-Year" after last winter's racing campaign. Soon the track experts would think of Satan only as a sire, just as they did the Black. There was no doubt that the Black was already proclaimed by all as a great sire. He had given them the champions Satan and Bonfire and Black Minx, and in the paddocks back at the farm were other colts and fillies, all promising in their own right.

But for a while, Alec thought, I can forget all that. Now the Black can be just another horse, roaming at will and running as he was born to run. No duties, no routines, no schedules.

Suddenly their steady flight was disturbed. The plane bucked, almost sending Alec out of his seat. There was a scrambling of the Black's hoofs as he sought to keep his balance. The plane leveled off, only to lurch again a few moments later. Alec left his seat to go to the Black's head. He was quieting him when the compartment door opened and the captain came inside.

"There's a storm to our south," he said. "We're skirting the edges of it. Had to change our course and come up more to the north."

"Where are we now?" asked Alec.

"Over western Nebraska. I doubt that the weather will get any rougher than it is now, but maybe you'd better sit down and fasten your seat belt."

"No, I'd better stick close to him," Alec said.

"Is he all right?"

Alec nodded. "Just a little uneasy."

After the captain left, Alec stayed close to the Black, talking to him constantly as the plane's bucking continued. For over an hour it went on, and the Black didn't like it. He had trouble keeping his feet, and his eyes were bright and startled.

Alec became uneasy. He knew the pilots were doing their best to keep the plane steady, that there was nothing to fear from the weather itself. But the Black was getting worked up. His head felt damp, and his small ears flicked back and forth. Alec felt the mounting warmth of his great body through the blankets that covered him.

He sought to comfort him, using every trick he knew. It wasn't that he was afraid the Black would break completely out of control. He was more worried about the moistness of his head, the heat of his body. A hot horse in a cool, drafty plane could result in complications. He rubbed the stallion's muzzle, trying to get him to stick out his tongue in play. But the Black would have none of it now. The floor of the plane suddenly dropped from beneath them, and the stallion's legs shifted again, spreading wide and trembling. Once more the plane steadied but additional harm had been done. The Black snorted and shook his head, pulling hard against the tie ropes. His long forelock was damp with sweat.

Alec drew the blankets higher on the Black's neck. He talked to him, remembering to ask, not demand. He pleaded with him in their own special way. He sought the stallion's complete attention, his confidence, quietly reassuring him that there was nothing to fear. And slowly, very slowly, his soft sounds and movements had their effect upon the great stallion. The Black shook his head less often, and his body, though still hot, ceased to tremble. He stopped pulling on the ropes and kept his legs wide apart, waiting and ready for the next sickening drop of the plane. His eyes remained on Alec.

The captain came back again. "I'm sorry," he said. "It was worse than I'd expected it to be. But we're just about out of it now. Is everything all right with you?" He looked at the Black's glistening head with uneasy eyes.

"It was rough for a while, but he's all right now, I think," Alec said. "Where are we?"

"Over western Wyoming. The Rockies are just ahead, so we'll be climbing. Come up forward when you get a chance, and take a good look at the country. It's really rugged, but beautiful."

When he was alone once more, Alec felt the plane's ascent as the pressure in his ears increased. The flight was now smooth, and the Black quiet. He wiped the stallion as dry as he could, and put another blanket on him to keep him warm. Then, knowing that his horse was thirsty, he went to the ten-gallon can of water he had brought along, and poured a little into a pail. He tested it to make certain it was as warm as he wanted it. Nothing cold should go into the Black's stomach now.

It took only a few swallows for the stallion to finish the water Alec offered him. Then he whinnied, shoving his slender nostrils against the side of the pail. He was heated. He wanted more.

"In a little while you can have it," Alec said, "but not now."

There was a new note to the engines. The humming rose to a greater pitch as the plane slanted ever upward. Alec sat down in his bucket seat. The Black was quiet. There was nothing more for him to do.

The door of the forward compartment opened, and the copilot said, "The captain would like you to come up and take a look at what's ahead of us."

"Thanks, but I don't want to leave him alone."

The copilot came inside. "I'd be glad to sit with him a few minutes. It would be something to tell my kids, that I was baby-sitting the Black tonight."

Alec smiled and turned to the stallion. The Black's eyes were half closed. It would be safe to leave him. He got to his feet. "Okay," he said, "I'll just take a quick look and come right back."

He left the compartment door open in order to catch any sound from the Black, any call from the copilot. Ahead, he saw the captain's silhouette against the lighted instrument panel. Outside the great windshield were the mountains. The air was like polished crystal, and a full moon brought out in sharp relief the towering and jagged peaks that reared in the night sky.

The captain kept the plane in its steady climb. "Sit down over there," he said, motioning to the copilot's seat. "Ahead of us is the Wind River Range."

Below the jumbled mass of rock, Alec could see the endless woods with their deep gullies and ridges. The land looked so wild and desolate. Yet every once in a while, he could make out the few lights of scattered towns, and occasionally, too, the pinpoints of a car's headlights moving along some mountain road.

The captain was telling him to look at an avalanche scar on a peak just ahead of them, when Alec heard the sharp ring of a pail striking metal. He turned quickly, and then got up, hurriedly leaving the compartment.

The copilot was setting the water pail to one side of the stall when Alec reached him. The boy turned to the Black and touched him, to find his lips cold and dripping. His own stomach churned as he reached for the pail.

"He was thirsty," the copilot was saying. "He drank a whole pailful."

Alec didn't look at him. He tested what little water was left in the pail. *Ice cold!* He flicked a glance at the water cooler at the far end of the plane. That's where the copilot had gotten it. Ice-cold water, the worst thing the Black could have had at this time.

"I'm sure going to have something to tell the kids when I get home," the copilot added. "Everyone in the neighborhood will know that I tended the Black. Well, I'll get back now. Thanks a lot for letting me stay with him."

Alec said nothing. His eyes never left the Black. In five or ten minutes he'd know if the worst was going to happen. Fifteen minutes at the most. His heart pounded, choking the breath from him. Cramp colic always came soon and suddenly, if it came at all. He'd seen horses with it before, horses with careless handlers who had given their charges long drinks of cold water when the animals were warm, or had ridden them, when heated, through deep streams or cold rains. The result was spasms of the small intestines, causing intense pain. Although most painful, this form of colic was scarcely ever fatal if one had the services of a veterinarian to give injections that would stop the pain, and one was able to walk his horse, keeping him on his feet, so he could not roll and rupture his stomach or bowels.

But what could he do here in the confines of this plane, thousands of feet above a mountainous wilderness? *If cramp colic did come, what would he do?*

He felt his self-confidence ebbing. He stood there, watching the Black, hoping desperately that nothing was going to happen. Angrily, he shook off his feeling of helplessness. Going to the tack trunk, he took out a bottle of medicine he had used before on colicky horses while awaiting the arrival of a veterinarian. He removed another blanket and a bottle of liniment, placing them on top of the trunk, and then he went back to the stallion. The Black was quiet, even drowsing. Perhaps . . . He looked at his watch. Ten minutes had gone by. He left the Black to go quickly into the pilots' compartment.

They had their backs to him, the copilot wearing his radio headset. They did not know he was there until he said, "I might have a sick horse."

Surprised by his presence, they turned simultaneously. "Sick?" the captain asked, studying Alec's face. "How sick?"

"Bad, if it comes at all."

"Then he isn't sick now?"

"No."

"How do you know he will be?"

"I don't know for sure. But you'd better get to the nearest airport anyway."

The captain tried to smile. "You're kidding. We're over the roughest part of the trip."

"I'm not kidding," Alec said. "It's cramp colic, and if it comes I won't be able to control him."

"You mean . . ." The captain stopped, his face turning white. "How long do we have?"

"A matter of minutes now, longer only if I can keep control." Alec's eyes met the captain's. "We've got to get down."

Turning away, the captain opened the throttle and kicked the plane hard to the right. Through the windshield Alec saw the spinning peaks below.

"Give me an hour," the captain said. "I'll need an hour. There's a small airport behind us." He turned to his copilot. "Get them on the radio. Tell them we'll be coming in, and why."

"Yes, sir."

Alec returned to the Black. The stallion had his small head raised. He whinnied as Alec came toward him. He put out his tongue. Alec pulled it, then let go.

A few minutes went by with Alec praying that he was all wrong, that nothing was going to happen. He was conscious of the racing engines and in silent prayer urged them to still greater speed. Only when he and the Black were on the ground would his deathly fear leave him. With or without a veterinarian's services he'd have a chance there. On the ground he might be able to work the pain out of the stallion. But not up here. Here, if it came, the results would be fatal to all of them.

For another minute it was quiet except for the roaring engines, and then the Black stopped his tongue play to stamp his feet impatiently. He pulled on the tie ropes, trying to turn his head to look *at his stomach.*

Alec's face turned pale. Here were the first symptoms of cramp colic! *"No, boy, no,"* he said. Tears came to his eyes, and he roughly brushed them away. He rubbed the Black's muzzle. The stallion stomped again, harder this time. The pains had begun; they'd get more severe with every successive minute now.

Alec turned away, opened the compartment door, and shouted, "It's started!" He closed the door, not knowing if they'd heard him, and realizing it didn't matter. The pilots were doing all they could to get to an airport. The rest was solely up to him. He got the bottle of medicine from the trunk and returned to the Black's head. The pain was beginning to show in the stallion's eyes. They were large and bright, the pupils dilating more and more.

Alec was careful with the medicine. Seldom had it been necessary to give the Black any drugs, and never had it been easy. Talking to the stallion, he moved to the side of his head, letting the fingers of one hand creep up to the Black's mouth. In his other hand he had the bottle, holding it low to keep the stallion from seeing it while he opened his mouth. He was bringing it up when the Black tossed his head, striking Alec's hand and sending the bottle crashing against the floor. It was the only colic medicine Alec had.

The Black struggled as the spasms increased in their violence. He plunged, and the tie ropes strained but held. He pawed furiously, and then tried to get down to roll, straining the ropes again. Through the heavy blankets covering him came large and ever-widening splotches of sweat.

Alec ran to get more dry blankets and the liniment. Returning to the Black, he threw the blankets over the heaving body to induce more perspiration; then, unmindful of his own safety, he went inside the close stall and began rubbing liniment on the stallion's stomach.

The Black was beside himself with pain. He knew no master, no love or tolerance, nothing but the terrible spasms that racked his stomach. He sought to rid himself of them by violent action. His thin, delicate head was wrought with veins that were bulging, almost bursting with his heated blood. He snorted, gathering himself back on his haunches as if for a mighty leap. His body quivered, and froth showered from gaping mouth and nostrils.

"*Black . . . oh, Black. I'm sorry, sorry . . .*" But Alec's words, repeated over and over in his terrible misery, went unheard. Pain had closed the stallion's eyes and ears, blinding him, deafening him to all he knew and loved.

Suddenly the Black flung himself forward, and the stall door latch gave way beneath his great strength and weight. The tie ropes held, but his halter broke at the buckle, and the leather hung loosely upon his head. He stood still for a moment, not realizing he was free.

Alec ran to the door of the pilot's compartment and, opening it, shouted, *"Get down, down! Now!"*

He shut the door again, and turned to find the Black bolting forward in a mighty leap. His loose blankets caught on the stall door but his momentum carried him on, rending straps, buckles and fabric. The plane suddenly lurched beneath his heavy movements. He careened against the opposite side, and came away to throw himself on the floor, his naked body sweating and squirming.

The plane bucked violently, lunging crazily to one side, then up and down. It stopped with a sudden jar, leveled off, then quickly slanted down.

Alec knew fear, all-engulfing fear at the abrupt descent. His chest was tight, his mouth slack and gaping. If he didn't do something, if he didn't go to his horse now, he'd never go. He took a step, then another toward the Black.

The stallion got to his feet and reared, striking his head against the top of the plane. He whirled as he came down, and threw himself on the floor again, his legs thrashing above him.

Alec was flung hard against the side of the plane as it lurched once more with the Black's ponderous rolling. The engines shrilled a new sound, an ever-expanding, protesting roar in the night, and the floor slanted downward more steeply. Alec picked himself up. He realized that the pilots, blinded by fear themselves, were going down for any kind of a landing while they still had control of the plane. But not on a runway, not at an airport. They were still too far away. There was only a mountain wilderness beneath them!

He staggered toward the Black and found himself looking into eyes that were dull and heavy. The stallion's breathing grew louder and louder until it could be heard even above the roar of the engines. Alec reached for him.

Suddenly the stallion's eyes came open with a snap, and once more they were wild in their brightness. He struggled to his feet, his nostrils swelling and widening. A spasm wracked his great body. He bolted, plunging the whole length of the compartment before losing his balance and falling again.

The plane bounced in the sky, its engines rising and dwindling in horrible protest. Alec was hurled against the compartment door. For a moment he lay there, knowing there was nothing he could do. The door moved against his back, and then a voice shouted, "We're crash landing. Get some blankets around you!"

Alec picked himself up, only to be thrown off his feet again as the plane slewed to the left, and then down, ever down. Now he crawled past the rolling body of the stallion. He pulled himself to the door and unlocked it. They were riding a comet toward a blackened earth. The only thing he could do now was to provide an escape for them, if they landed safely. He glanced out the window and saw a knife-edged ridge below them. Were they to cut a swath through the trees or was there a clearing beyond?

The Black was on his feet and moving about again. Alec pressed himself hard against the side of the plane to avoid the flaying, frenzied hoofs of his horse. The plane grazed the treetops. "Get her up!" he tried to shout. But why? What chance did the pilots have to find a safe place to land? There was nothing to do but wait, wait for the staggering plane to find its way into the earth so close below them.

It seemed to come with the crash of the Black's body against the floor. The plane leaped and jolted, trying to free itself from the trees that sought to clutch and gather it to them. Knowing the crash was coming, Alec pushed against the door to provide an escape for them. It went hard at first, then suddenly burst wide open with a roar of wind. He glimpsed the tops of trees just below, then something snatched him from his feet, tearing him forever from the heaving floor of the plane. *He was outside and falling.* His last conscious thought was a realization that the plane had lifted again, clearing the trees as if in final, angry repulsion of them. Its engines thundered, rising and dwindling, as its dark bulk went on without him.

Then came the tearing and crashing of his body into the trees. He screamed and his arms flayed wildly. An explosion came, and he knew nothing more but blackness.

The Unknown

4

It was hard . . . hard . . . so hard. Yet, finally, he was
able to open his eyes. There was nothing for him to see,
only darkness. He didn't care, and closed his eyes again.
Slowly, ever so slowly, he was able to raise a hand to his
head. He knew it had to be his head, not from touch, but
because of the terrible pain that began there and descended and racked his body. He located the great
swelling on the crown of his head, but resting his hand
there afforded him no relief from the intensity of his pain.
He kept his eyes closed, seeking sleep to soothe him and
provide solace.

Sleep did not come, could not overcome this great
barrier of pain. He tried opening his eyes again. His lids
came apart slowly because even that slight movement
served only to increase his suffering. He made a great

effort, trying to withstand the horrible electric shocks that seemed to be passing through him. When he was able to see again he kept his eyes open, knowing he could not sleep, and tried to think.

Where was he?

His fingers found the bark of the tree beside him. Yes, it was a tree. But why was it so wet, so moist and clammy beneath his touch? He drew back his hand, putting it to his mouth, and tasted his own raw and bleeding flesh. Something had happened, something horrible. But what? Fiery currents tortured him while he tried to think, to remember. Quickly he forced these thoughts from his mind to ease the pain. He used his ears then, hoping they would furnish him with all he wanted to know, *needed to know,* if he was to get assistance.

He squinted his eyes to shut out some of the pain. He listened, and heard wind roaring through treetops. Yes, there were trees all around him. He was certain of that now. And it was night . . . that, too, he knew. He heard the scream of an animal, and to him, just then, it was all the more wild and terrible because it rent the night air of an unknown wilderness. Yet when the scream trailed away, he thought no more of it, so wretched was his pain. Instead he listened to another sound, something that moved beneath the cry of wind and trees, something that rushed like the wind, but at a lower and more gentle pitch. It came to him suddenly that the sound could be made by a stream. He opened his eyes a little more.

He lay in a gully, and the ground sloped away from him. The low, rushing sound came from beyond. The way to it must be downgrade with nothing to climb. Yet he hesitated, not wanting to move, dreading the pain he knew any movement would bring.

Reaching for the trunk of the tree behind him, he dug his nails into its bark, and began pulling himself to his feet. He screamed in his agony, stopped, and held fast to the tree, not wanting to lose the few feet he had already gained. He pulled again until, staggering and weak, he stood on trembling legs. For a few minutes he rested, then he pushed himself away from the tree.

He fell forward more often than he walked. Yet he never stopped in his search for the stream, for he knew he'd never go on again if he did. With every step, the agonizing pain mounted until he thought his head would burst. Yet he went on, sometimes on hands and knees, always moving a little closer to the sound of running water. He tried to think of the comfort the water would bring to his head. He tried to concentrate on this and nothing more.

Finally he came to it, a thread of a stream rushing down the mountainside. He crawled into it, heedless of the sharp rocks that tore his hands and knees, opening fresh wounds, causing him to shed more blood.

He let his face fall into the cold water. The stream was shallow, and the stones at the bottom scraped his nose and mouth. He turned his head sideways, facing downstream. He lay there, letting the cold water run over his head. And for the first time his pain lessened. He had found his solace.

For a long, long while he lay there without moving,

without thinking. Then, suddenly, down the mountainside he saw the moving lights! With great effort he raised his head from the water. *Help was coming. Somebody knew. Somebody was coming for him!*

He staggered to his feet, and the pain beat his head again. It was severe but he was able to stand it now. It wasn't as bad as before. He would be able to move. He took a few steps, then stopped, his eyes on the lights below. They were no longer coming toward him, but turning away! They were not lights held in the hands of people coming to his aid, but the headlights of a car, a car that was moving along a mountain road, *not looking for him and even now leaving him behind.*

He screamed at the top of his voice, and this great effort caused him to drop to his knees and clutch his head. He didn't watch the car disappear down the road. His only thought was to get back to the stream, to let the cold, cold water ease his pain.

In time the pain lessened again, and while lying in the water he thought of the lights and the road below. He must reach it. Where one car had gone another could go. He needed help, needed it desperately. Not only to relieve him of his pain. No, not only that. There was something else, something he felt rather than knew. He felt that there was a barrier in his brain . . . a barrier that was shutting out the past. He couldn't explain it, but he knew nothing at all of who he was, or where he was, or what had happened. *He couldn't remember.*

After a long while, he raised his head from the water, and sat up. The pain returned, but he took hope from the fact that he could stand it better than before. He would be able to reach the road below. But before getting to his feet, he searched his clothes seeking some clue to his identity, and what had happened to him. He found a large amount of money in his pants pocket but no wallet, no papers, nothing that was of any help to him. Yet he had all this money, wet and soaked with blood.

He fingered the great tears in his shirt and pants. No, not really tears, but shreds of clothing scarcely covering his ravaged body. He must have been running, fighting his way through these woods for a long, long time. Crawling, too, by the sight of his raw hands and knees. But why? *Why?*

He sat there for some time, trying to think, trying to remember. But the insurmountable barrier in his brain kept its hold, reminding him that his mental searching was futile.

He was wearing only one shoe, and, leaning forward, he removed it to look inside for the name of a store, a city. There was nothing. He tore the collar from his shirt, looking for a label. He found one, and the name "McGregor." Was it just the brand name of the shirt or was it his name? He repeated the name over and over again, hoping it would break down the terrible mental barrier. But nothing came of it, only greater despair, and more pain.

Once again he put his head in the cold water, seeking relief. Eventually he got to his feet and, stumbling, moved down the mountainside. He must reach the road below. Get help. *Someone* would know who he was, and what had happened to him.

He followed the rushing stream for a long while, turning when it turned, afraid to leave the solace it afforded him. Finally he had to abandon it in order to reach the road below. Heavier woods were before him, solid and alive, and he plunged into their vastness, alternately staggering and crawling. Brush wrapped its arms about him, pulling him down only to let him go again as he rolled with the steep grade, refusing to stop, knowing the road beyond was his only salvation.

How long it had been since he had left the stream he didn't know. It seemed an eternity. His pain was intense, and there was no stream now to comfort him. He had to go on. His squinting eyes looked for the lights that would tell him he was near his goal. But none came for a long while. Then he saw them far away, winding their way with the contour of the mountain. He screamed, and tried to run. A black bulk rose in front of him, and he went down hard, his hands finding the base of a tree. He pulled himself to his knees and, still screaming, began to crawl. Now the lights were close to him. A hundred yards away? He got to his feet, screaming again at the top of his voice. But with the lights came a roar, the thunderous roar of a heavy truck that made his cries seem pitifully soft in comparison. Forgetful of his pain he ran again, faster than before, and when he crashed into another tree he stayed down for a long while.

When he opened his eyes again he knew that the truck has passed. He crawled toward the road. Soon he would reach it. He would lie there, waiting for other headlights to find him, to stop, to give him peace. He reached the road on will alone, and stretched the full length of his agonized body upon it. There was nothing more to do but wait. If only he could sleep while he waited!

He had his head turned sideways, his eyes closed. He didn't know what made him try to open them again, but he was aware that when he did they formed two narrow slits in his cut and swollen face. He looked up the road, and a convulsion wracked his body. Ahead were the red taillights of the truck! And beside the right front wheel a flashlight moved. He heard the sound of tools being thrown into a metal kit.

He tried to scream but had no strength left for the effort. Once more he started crawling. He saw the flashlight go off, and then came the slam of the cab's door.

The tire had been fixed. The truck was going!

He staggered to his feet simultaneously with the sudden roar of the engine. He managed to run, weaving from one side of the road to the other, his eyes on the truck, his hands stretched out to it. He brought forth a pitiful scream from his constricted throat.

He was so close to it! A few yards now, a few more feet. But the truck was already moving, and its backboards were eluding his groping fingers. The heavy canvas which covered the back of the truck flapped in the wind as though waving good-by to him.

With a last, desperate effort he let all his weight fall forward, his hands stretched out. If they grasped nothing he would stay on the road forever. . . .

The boards were beneath his hands! He closed his fingers and held on to them, his legs no longer carrying him. After a moment his dragging, burning feet forced him to exert himself again. Slowly he raised them until he got one on the lowest board. He waited, his breath coming in terrible gasps, then he brought up his other foot and stood on the back of the truck, his body pressed hard against the boards. Finally his hand went to a corner of the canvas flap. He pulled it aside, his eyes trying to penetrate the blackness of the interior. He'd get in there. He would walk forward until he reached the back of the cab. He would tell the driver that he was there, that he needed him.

Every movement was one of horrible pain, but he got his body over the boards and let it fall under the canvas siding. He struck a large box, and now he realized that the truck was fully loaded, that there was no chance of his reaching the cab. Well, there was a place for him to lie down, anyway. He would stay there until the truck stopped again. He was safe. He had found help. He closed his eyes, and sleep came to him.

Miles upon miles rolled beneath the wheels of the long trailer truck. While one man drove, the other slept, and they alternated without stopping for even a moment. One would move from behind the big steering wheel while the other took it over, sliding into the seat from a bunk in the back of the cab. One man's foot would leave the accelerator to be replaced promptly by the other's. They were hardened drivers, with many thousands of miles and many years on the road behind them. Their world was this cab in which they had spent the greater part of their adult lives. Seldom did their eyes turn to the flats or canyons or mountains through which they passed. Only the road held their attention, the never-ending road that was their sole interest and life.

They traveled through the rest of the night, conscious only of each other's snores, the road itself and the steady beat of the powerful engine. Ever southward they traveled, their experienced eyes aware of every twist and turn, every downgrade and climb, but never noticing the natural wonders about them, never seeing the moonlight baring the beautiful tints of the mountain ranges through which they passed. They were too busy, and their eyes too deadened by the road to see mountain ranges as anything but obstacles in their way, to be climbed and left behind.

With the coming of dawn, they had left Wyoming and were in Utah. They stopped early for breakfast, but within a very few minutes were on their way again. They were anxious to reach Nevada and get rid of their cargo. Yet they knew that no sooner would the huge trailer be emptied than it would be filled again, and their long trip back to Chicago would begin.

All day long they pushed the truck hard, and only when night fell did they stop again to eat. Almost grudgingly they left the cab to go into a roadside diner and sit down at the counter. Glancing at the menu, one said, "I guess it's the beef stew for me."

The other looked up at the counterman. "Beef stew for two," he said. "An' make it fast. We're in a hurry."

Impatiently they awaited their orders. When their overloaded plates were put before them they began eating, paying no attention to anyone else in the diner or to the conversation that was taking place.

The counterman said to the customer a few stools away from them, "They haven't found any trace of that kid and his horse yet."

"Yeah, so I heard on the radio," the customer replied. "But they'll find them, all right. They got all kinds of planes looking, even helicopters."

"I ain't so sure they will," the counterman said. "That's rough country, that part of Wyoming is. Some say it's the worst in the States."

The customer nodded his head gravely. "I heard the kid and his horse started for the north. How'd they know that?"

"The pilots said so. After they got the plane down in the clearing they went back an' found the door open. They saw the horse taking off in a northerly direction."

"An' the kid?"

"He was riding him. It was pretty dark, but they could see the kid on him."

"Sure funny they'd take off like that."

"Yeah, but that's the way it happened," the counterman said. "It's lucky the pilots themselves got help by this morning."

"Well, they had their radio. No reason why they shouldn't have."

"I guess so."

The counterman got some coffee for the truckdrivers who had shouted at him, and then returned. "You know all about that horse, don't you?" he asked his customer.

"Only what I heard. He's called the Black . . . a race horse or something. Pretty well known, isn't he?"

"I should say so," the counterman replied quickly. "He's a great—or at least he was at one time—a great race horse. Now he's a famous sire."

"A what?"

"A sire, I said. Say, don't you ever follow the races?"

"No."

"Well, anyway, the Black fathered Satan . . . and Satan's a champion."

"Oh," said the customer. "Well, all I hope is that they find the kid."

"Sure," agreed the counterman. "That's all I care about, too."

The customer left his stool. "I don't think we need to worry much about him. That part of Wyoming may be desolate, but at least he's got a horse under him. A good horse can find his way out of a lot of jams that people couldn't."

The counterman used his cleaning rag. "Yeah," he said, "and what a horse, the best there is!"

"Hey, you!"

The counterman turned quickly to the two truckdrivers. "Coming, gentlemen," he said.

"Give us a check," one said.

"Yes, *sir*." He wanted no trouble with these men.

The truckdrivers left the diner and, climbing into their cab, drove off into the night. In the back of the trailer, Alec Ramsay still slept. Many more miles piled up behind him, taking him ever farther away from Wyoming and the great search that had begun for him and the Black.

The Search

5

An hour after the plane had come down in its forced landing, the black stallion moved slowly through the woods. Crazed by his colic cramps, he had entered the woods in full gallop, seeking relief by speed and violent action. But the darkness and the density of the trees had slowed him to a walk. He'd sweated and pawed in his frustration. He had wanted to run and, failing that, to lie down and roll and kick. He'd found he could do neither, for the woods were solid and alive with thickly grown trees, giving him room only to wind his way among them. Thus, he had been forced to stay on his feet, to walk . . . and this light exercise, more than anything else, had brought his cramps to an end.

He forgot his pains quickly. Now his small, fine head was raised high, sniffing the air, his nostrils quivering.

He continued walking in a northerly direction, his ears pointed and alert to new and strange sounds . . . monotonous and low scraping notes, sharp staccato calls, and, in the distance, a forlorn and dismal howl. The howl came again, wailing in the wind. He was interested, but unafraid. He had known the great solitude of the wild in another land. Now he was entering a new and strange and beautiful country, but it held no terrors for him. He was alone and free. He remembered nothing of his domestic life, of barns or farms, or a boy who loved him. Before him was a world as thrilling, exciting, and as wild as he.

Presently he came out of the woods to more open country. Yet he did not break from his walk, for the land before him was rocky and crisscrossed with gorges and canyons. For a long while he carefully made his way about the splintered rock that was merciless to his unshod feet. He came to a stop in a low walled canyon, and his gaze traveled to the long black line of trees above the bared rims and crags of stone. He turned his head back in the direction from which he'd come.

He stood as still as the stone about him. For some time he kept sniffing the air; then he began walking again. No longer did he travel to the north, but back to the south. He entered a cleft in another canyon that took him through rotting cliffs. It cut down deep into the earth, and his path was strewn with gravel and rocks. Yet he never faltered, for his wild instinct told him this new trail would take him to the softer country beyond.

An hour later he came to the woods again, but at a point much farther away than where he had entered the gutted terrain. His great body trembled in his excitement at being able to choose any trail that beckoned him. He listened to the wind as it roared and lulled through the trees. He began climbing, his unerring instinct telling him of the pure running water and succulent grasses of the wilder ranges above. He was aware of the gray shadows that trailed him during his ascent. He was wary, but unafraid. He had the utmost confidence in his speed and endurance and cunning.

Throughout the rest of the night he traveled ever upward, and the air became clearer, sharper. Yet his climb was a gradual one, never steep. The pine trees still hemmed him in, affording him no outlook from his mountain threshold. It was almost morning when he came to the small meadow so typical of those he had known in the high country of his desert homeland. His shrill neigh echoed the profound joy that shook his body. He ran for the first time in many hours, and his long limbs carried him beautifully and swiftly across the carpet of short, thick grass.

Finally he stopped running to taste the pure water from rushing streams, to savor the cold air in his nostrils, and then finally to graze upon the wild grasses he loved. The few hours left of the night were spent on a bed of these grasses, fresh and sweet scented. He rested with eyes closed, but his ears and nostrils remained alert, ready to catch the slightest noise or faintest scent.

With the first hour of grayness he was on his way once more, leaving the mountain valley to its solitude. High above him rose range after range, tier upon tier of cloud-shattering peaks, some snow-clad, and others bare and sheer. But the stallion had no use for the world above the timberline, a world consisting only of rock and snow and sky.

He trotted easily through the great woods, his hoofs making no sound on the springy cushion of pine needles. He no longer was slowed to a walk, for with the light of day he was able to choose his way easily through the aisles of trees. Why he ran when he had nowhere to go didn't puzzle him. He ran because he loved to run, and some natural instinct kept him traveling ever southward. Flocks of birds rose from the thickets with a clatter. But he paid little attention to them, never slackening his easy strides.

Several hours later he came to an open plateau and stopped to graze upon the bleached mountain grass. Suddenly, alert, he raised his head, holding long blades of the grass between his lips. Only his ears had caught the movement of his foe, for it was downwind. He whirled to meet the headlong rush of an enemy from the cover of the woods.

The trumpet roar of the bull moose was low and guttural at first. Quickly it rose to a high-pitched scream, only to descend to the roar again, and end with a grunt. He charged, his heavy antlers cleaving the air in their great spread and length.

The stallion took one look at this strange body that came hurtling toward him, a body taller than his own and made more startling by the thick, bony slabs that were pointed his way. He knew better than to rise and clash in deadlock with that horned head. Instead, he sprang swiftly away, avoiding the low-charging attack. He threw himself on the yellowish gray back in violent assault, hoping by his weight alone to bring it to the ground. But his foe began slipping away from him, so with raking teeth the stallion bit deeply into the moose's dark brown neck, ripping and tearing. As he moved off, his feet slipped, and before he could right himself, the horned head had slashed his belly. He screamed, whirled, and let fly his hind legs, landing so hard a blow that it sent his enemy down and rolling.

With savage speed he attacked again, his pounding forefeet seeking the rolling body. Again he landed crushing, pommeling blows, but his foe came up, and its pointed head found his flesh again. The stallion felt more pain and his fury mounted. His eyes were blood-red as he flung himself full upon his opponent. With crashing forefeet he battered it across the back of its neck, unmindful now of his own pain. Again he lodged his teeth into ravaged flesh.

Yet once more his foe succeeded in heaving up beneath him, forcing him to relinquish his hold and fall backward. He rolled on the ground, feeling the long horns after him, searching to rip open his stomach. Only the uncanny agility he had inherited from his desert forebears saved him then. He avoided the plunging head, and got to his feet. Now he was terrible in his cunning. He circled his foe warily, feinted and attacked from behind and from the side, avoiding altogether those sharp bony prongs that had already ripped open his body. He was watchful every second, waiting for his enemy to stumble, to be caught off guard. Then he would launch his assault.

With the black stallion using all of his cunning and strength, the end came quickly. No animal of the wild country could have met an adversary so worthy, so ruthless. The great bull moose knew this now that it was too late. He coughed, the choking cough of death. And with the sound of it, the black stallion came in again for a fresh and final assault. He feinted to the front, and the moose's head went down to fend him off. The stallion swerved and dealt his foe a blow from the side, sending him staggering. Then he reared and his powerful forelegs came down together, splitting the bull moose's skull.

For a moment the Black stood over the great body beneath him, and his loud, clarion call of conquest was heard for the first time in those regions. He went to the edge of the plateau. Before him was an abrupt, sheer drop of many thousands of feet to lower country. He stood there, his body bleeding from his wounds, his breath coming fast from his combat. He looked below at the canyons, then up and beyond, taking in the range upon range of mountains with their great woods and peaks, all that mysterious, wild country which seemed to have no end. As though in warning to its inhabitants, he screamed his high-pitched battle cry once more, and the great wilderness echoed his call, resounding from the mountainsides until the very air was alive with the ring of it. When finally it was still, he set out again, traveling as before to the south.

Back over the many miles the black stallion had come during the long night and part of a day, back to the clearing where the crippled plane lay, the search for Alec Ramsay and his horse was in progress. Already two local planes were flying low, winging their way over knife-edged ridges whose slopes and peaks loomed large in the windshields. The pilots had flown searches before above these desolate mountain ranges. They crisscrossed diligently, their eyes leaving the ground below only long enough to enable them to rudder hard and away from the menacing shoulder peaks.

Yet this time the pilots were not looking for the bright winking of metal from a crashed plane, nor for a swath cut among the treetops. No, this time it was even more difficult, for this country could swallow up a boy and a horse without a sign, a trace.

One pilot slanted down into the deep canyons. Only here, away from sheltered trees, did he have a chance of seeing them. Yet even this could not be called open country. There were too many crags and clefts, too many black gullies and canyons. His great hope was that the boy would see him, that he would be given some signal that they were there, and waiting to be found.

He told himself that this was not a futile search, that he or one of the many other pilots who would join the search within a few hours would certainly find the boy and horse. They must be somewhere below, their eyes on the sky, looking for him. If only they would give him some sign to tell him where they were!

He kept to the canyon country, leaving the great wooded mountainside to the other plane. He twisted and turned with the steep walls, kicking his plane hard away from them only to be confronted by the rising, forbidding mountains that hemmed in these canyons. For hours he climbed and dropped, and the afternoon slipped away as an increasing sense of futility mounted within him.

Finally he rose again and held his plane at cruising speed. He began circling, and noticed that the other plane was now doing the same. They had given up baring their wings and lives to the sides of the mountains. Now they would cruise and watch for a sign, a signal from below that would tell them where to go.

Certainly if the boy were alive he must see them searching for him. *And if he wasn't* . . . The thought only added to the pilot's weariness. The pattern then, he knew, would be the familiar one of long searches on foot rather than from the sky. Long days and weeks of searching, perhaps without finding a trail, a clue, anything at all in this vast wilderness. But the ground search, although heartbreaking and futile, would be necessary because of relatives left behind, and the newspapers that demanded it. If this were settled country it would be different. There'd be some hope then. But it wasn't settled. In every direction it was an unexplored wilderness, feared and avoided by hunters and trappers, *by all*.

The pilot thought of the wild animals who stalked these ranges, the mountain lions and bears, the wolf packs and coyotes. Any of these could have attacked and killed the horse during the night. And if the horse had gone down what chance had the boy?

These thoughts drove him down to the treetops again, and he brushed his wings against them until the sunlight disappeared behind the highest of the western ranges.

For a brief period he carried on his relentless search in the golden afterglow of the sun shedding its light from behind the peaks. Finally this light went, and it became dark. He banked his plane for home. Other planes would join the search tonight and tomorrow. Tomorrow, perhaps tomorrow, they would find them . . . or even tonight.

While the planes had been searching from the sky, two woodsmen followed the Black's trail from the crippled plane. By sunset they came to the rocky country and there they stopped to kneel on the ground, looking at the large, almost oval hoofprints that were there. Finally one said, "Take a look, Milt, these are the last ones we're goin' to see of his."

The other man said nothing, only raising his head to look ahead at the desolate and tortuous terrain: miles upon miles of bare, gutted rock, spreading into the great woods where no horse, not even a shod one, would leave a track.

"He's gone to the north, all right," the first man spoke again, "just like they thought."

Picking up his rifle, the other turned. "Come on, Luke. We ain't goin' on with no tracks to follow. We'll go back and tell 'em so. Let someone else decide what to do. We gets paid to track."

"An' there ain't no tracks no more," Luke said, following.

The airliner was hours out of New York City, yet no word had passed between Henry Dailey and Alec's father. The tragic news, coming early that morning, had drained them spiritually and emotionally. They were two old men and there was nothing left for either without Alec.

Henry put his hand on Mr. Ramsay's knee. "We've got to believe he's alive," he said.

"Do *you* believe it, Henry?" Mr. Ramsay's words could hardly be heard. "The reporters . . . they said the search has been going on since last night." His trembling hands went to his face to cover it, and sobs wracked his long, thin body.

"We got to believe he's alive. We got to." Henry was silent for a long time, but his hand never left his friend's knee. Finally he said, "Remember, Alec's got the Black with him. Remember that, Bill."

Mr. Ramsay's voice was muffled by his hands, but Henry heard him say, "Thank God for that. Thank God. It's our only hope." Then his hands came away, and his glazed eyes found Henry's. Bitterness crept into his voice. "But why did he take Alec away? Why didn't Alec stay in the plane? Why?"

Henry couldn't face those eyes. He turned away. "I don't know, Bill. The horse was in bad trouble. A colic attack, from what I can make out of what the reporters told us. Maybe Alec was trying to help him after the plane came down. I don't know."

Neither said anything more. The sky darkened with the swift coming of night, *another* night. Henry tried to close his ears to the sobs from the seat beside him. "I've got to keep believing they're alive," he told himself. "If I don't I'm goin' to be no good to them or myself. They're out there tonight, alive, and waiting to be found. They're out there *together*. Remember that, and I'll be all right. *They're together.*"

But the Black was spending his second night high on a southern range, many miles away from where they were looking for him. Still farther to the south, and in another state, Alec Ramsay was awakening from his long sleep in the back of the rumbling trailer truck.

The Long Night

6

The truck swerved abruptly, throwing him against a corner of one of the wooden boxes. He felt the wheels leave the road, riding crazily on what must have been soft and deep-rutted shoulders, and then the truck began slowing down. He got his feet beneath him, but before standing he touched the swelling on his head again. It was sore and throbbing, but the severe pain was gone. His sleep had helped. How long had he been riding? It wasn't important.

All that mattered was that he was afraid to ask himself, *"Who am I? What has happened to me?"*

He was afraid because he knew he still did not know the answers. And just now he did not want to disturb this peace, this comfort which came with the relief from his violent pain. So he thought only of the slowing truck, and pulled himself upright.

Opening the back canvas, he looked out into the night, its darkness broken only by the white road that trailed like a ribbon. On either side of it were mountains. The same mountains, the same night, he believed. The truck came to a stop, and he raised a foot to the boards. He felt the severe pain again as he pulled his body upward. He tore his lips with his teeth, hoping this new torture would distract him from the old. He kept going, kept climbing.

A voice from far away said, "It ain't flat, Joe. It'll hold up for a while. Let's keep goin' until we hit the next station. Ain't no sense changin' it out here."

Hearing this, he screamed into the night and hung on to the top backboard, afraid to let go, afraid because of his terrible agony. He heard the heavy footsteps that came in answer to his scream. He felt the hands, as heavy as the feet had been, reach up to take him by the belt, and then he was pulled down.

For a moment he lay upon the road, his eyes closed. When he opened them two pairs of eyes were staring at him, and then two pairs of hands pulled him to his feet. It was hard focusing his eyes, harder still to move his swollen lips. And when he succeeded, his words came in gasps and were incoherent. They made no sense to the men who pulled him to the front of the truck to look at him in the glare of headlights.

The voice came to him again, an angry voice, rough, like the hands. "How long you hitched a ride with us? How long? Salt Lake City? Ain'tcha got eyes? Ya see that sign?"

He was pulled to his feet, and lifted brutally until his face was pressed hard against the truck's windshield.

There was a sign there, but he could not read it. The cold glass comforted his throbbing head.

"No riders, see! An' it means what it says, y'understan'? Do ya?" The hands shook him roughly. "You hitch a ride with us, an' we lose our jobs. Y'understan'? The Company's got spotters. Spotters, y'hear? They see ya, an' we get canned. Y'know that?"

The hands kept shaking him, and he knew he could stand no more. He tried to scream, but nothing came. "I . . . I . . . need he . . . help." His words were only whispers. "I want the police . . . need the police."

The two men were laughing, low, guttural laughs. They set him down on the side of the road, and he clung to the dirt, knowing aloneness again and the peace that came with it.

Out of the blackness he heard the harsh voice once more. "By the looks of ya I'd keep away from the police, if *I* were in your shoes."

The other voice came, "He ain't even got shoes. *His kind* ain't gonna' be helped by the cops none."

The cab door slammed, the engine roared, and they left him there. But he didn't care, didn't care at all.

How long he lay there, waiting for the pain to leave his head, he never knew. When he was able to sit up again he looked once more into darkness. Would this night ever end? Was it to last forever?

He sat still, knowing that only by keeping quiet would he have peace. He was on a valley road. Cars would come along, and perhaps one of them would stop. Someone would help him. Someone would take him to the police.

He'd tell them he couldn't remember anything, and they'd understand. He'd tell them that somehow he'd been struck on the head, and that was the reason he couldn't remember his name, or where he was, or what he'd been doing before he was hurt. They would help him. They might even be able to tell him who he was. Perhaps they had been looking for him. Perhaps . . .

The harsh voice came to him again, *"By the looks of ya I'd keep away from the police . . ."* He'd always remember that voice, those words.

By the looks of me? His torn hands felt his swollen face, felt the rags that should have been clothes, felt the clotted blood on his raw and open flesh. And finally they rested on the bulge in his pocket, and he remembered the large amount of money that was there. How had he come by so much money? Why had he been crawling through the woods, through a mountain wilderness? Had he been afraid? Had he been running from something? From the police?

Perhaps the police *were* looking for him. A new and terrifying fear gripped his body. Before he had been afraid for his life, afraid that the help he sought would not come. Now he felt the deadly fear of the *hunted.*

A car's headlights came down the road. He watched them with eyes that no longer sought aid and comfort. Instead they were shifting eyes seeking escape, the eyes of a fugitive!

He began crawling away from the side of the road, looking for tall grass, anything in which to hide. But it was open country, and he felt the headlights sweep down upon him. He lay flat and still, pressing his body close to the damp earth. He waited while the lights passed over him and then were gone.

He was getting up when he heard the screeching drag of braked wheels. He turned, and saw red taillights coming back toward him. He tried to get to his feet and run, but his legs wouldn't hold him. He sank back onto the ground. Better to take a chance. Better to lie and bluff his way along than to move and cause his pain to return again.

The car backed up until its headlights shone full upon him once more. Out of a long and racy convertible stepped a man. He was short in height, but big, tremendously big, about his shoulders and waist. He came waddling toward the boy, holding a revolver in his hand. When he stood over him, he put the gun away.

"Kid, are you hurt? What's happened to you?"

"I . . . I'd hitched a ride on a truck. The drivers threw me off here." He needed time, time to think and plan. He wanted to confide in no one just now. He didn't want to go to the police.

"And they beat you up?" The man didn't expect an answer. He was looking at the torn clothes, the swollen face. "Come on, kid. I'll help you," he added in great sympathy.

The boy was carried to the car, and when he had been set down he felt the softness of the upholstery against his head. It was good, so good, and his body relaxed. He felt safe with this man, safe and secure.

"Go to sleep," the fat man said kindly. "You look like

you could use it. Not many places open on this road, but the next time I stop for gas I'll let you know so you can clean up your face. That is, unless you think you should see a doctor, if I can find one. Do you feel any pain? Anything that might be broken?"

"No . . . no pain, nothing broken."

"Good. I'd sure like to get my hands on those guys. Beating up a kid! What's your name?"

What's your name? What's my name? What is my name? And he heard himself reply, "McGregor." The label on his ripped shirt had provided him with a name. "McGregor's my name," he said again.

"Scotch, eh? Mine's Washburn, Bill Washburn."

After that the fat man let him alone.

"McGregor's my name," he repeated to himself, closing his eyes. "It'll be my name until I can remember. I've been struck on the head. I have amnesia. Other people have had it and recovered. In time my memory will come back, and I'll know who I am. But now I'll keep all this to myself just in case . . . just in case I'm running away from something, *from the police.* There, I've said it and I feel better for having said it. My name is McGregor."

For the next two hours he pretended to be asleep. He knew any words would come hard from his lips, disjointed and rambling, making little sense most of the time. He didn't want to talk, not even to this man who was helping him get away. He'd only betray himself.

In time he felt the easing up of the powerful engine, and then there was gravel sliding beneath braked wheels. The car stopped, and the fat man's hand was on his shoulder.

"McGregor, I'm stopping for gas. You can get washed up here."

The boy slid out of the car and away from the lone overhead light near the gas pump. His head pains came back while he walked into the small station and found the door to the bathroom. He closed it quickly, locking it, and then he turned to the mirror. Beneath the bare, hanging bulb he looked at the face which belonged to him. His hair was red, dark red and matted with dried blood. His eyes had dark pupils and blue irises, but there were hundreds of tiny red veins streaking the whites. His nose was short, and looked small between his puffed and bruised cheeks. He had a wide mouth and large lips. Or were they swollen, too?

His glazed eyes traveled down the rest of his body. He carried all his weight in his shoulders and arms. Otherwise he was light, with a small waist, slender thighs and long legs. What use had he made of this body, these hands? He turned them up, looking at the palms. They were calloused and hard beneath the dried blood. His fingers were lean and strong. His hands had known work, hard work.

Turning on the water, he let it run over his head. The swelling on his crown throbbed, and it was sore to his touch. His headache was persistent, but once more the severe pains had subsided. He let the water run until it had washed his hair clean of all blood. He cupped it to his face with careful, gentle hands, and then he pushed back his hair, smoothing it down as best he could. When he had finished he looked far better except for his torn clothes and bare feet. But he could do nothing about those.

Before leaving the bathroom, he studied his face again. He wanted to know it, to remember it, for it belonged to him, *to McGregor*. He noticed the freckles on his nose and beneath his eyes, now that his face was clean. He saw, too, the thin white lines at the corners of his eyes, lines that came from squinting for long hours beneath a hot sun. His past life, he knew than, had been spent in the open. Doing what, though?

Hearing the incessant blaring of a horn, he left the bathroom to go to the car. He got inside without the station attendant's seeing him. Once more he lay back in the corner of the seat.

The fat man said while starting the engine, "You had me worried for a moment. I thought you might have decided not to come along." He laughed, but it was a kind laugh, the laugh of a person who liked people, all sorts of people. Yet curiosity was there, too, and it was reflected in his eyes and face. "You cleaned up fine," he said. "Does it make you feel better?"

McGregor only nodded.

The kid doesn't want to talk much, the fat man thought. Well, that was understandable. McGregor must have gone through a lot at the hands of those drivers. "I asked the gas station attendant if he knew of any doctors in this section," he said.

McGregor's eyes opened, and for a second the man thought he saw deep fear in them. "The guy laughed when I asked him," he went on. "Said the closest one was fifty miles back up the road and none going this way."

"Don't need a doctor," McGregor said.

For a while the fat man drove in silence, yet his gaze left the road often to glance at the huddled figure in the far corner. Finally he said, "Could you eat a sandwich? There are some right behind you."

When McGregor didn't reply, the man reached behind the seat himself and placed the box of sandwiches between them. "Help yourself," he said.

The road went across a flat stretch of country, and the car surged forward with increased speed beneath the heaviness of its driver's foot.

Yet the fat man took time to glance at the boy again when he heard the cover being removed from the box. He saw McGregor's glazed eyes turn toward him and then away, quickly, shiftily. He became a little worried about McGregor. Those eyes held more than pain. A haunted look was there . . . or was it more of a *hunted* look? He shrugged this disturbing thought from him. McGregor was only a kid, a poor kid who was bumming his way around the country. He had given rides to many of his kind. He had helped lots of them.

He said, "I always carry my own food when I drive all night, especially going through desolate country like this." He didn't look at McGregor. He knew the kid would eat if he kept his eyes off him.

"I'm interested in young people," he said jovially. "In fact, working for them is all I do now. I'm a retired building contractor. Retired two years ago, and thought

I'd go nuts not having anything to do. My wife couldn't see why I just couldn't take it easy. Sure, why not? Her life was going on pretty much as always in spite of my retirement. A wife's job doesn't change much when the old man retires, but *his* does."

The fat man paused, but he did not even glance at McGregor. He knew the boy was eating. "Less than a month of loafing, and I felt like a car with a new engine, all ready to go tearing down the road. But I had no place to go. I just moped around the house until one day I noticed that the kids in our town didn't have any place to play, and not much to do, either. I built an athletic field for them and a clubhouse. Then I went to another town and did the same kind of a job. Now I've been doing just that for two years. When youth organizations can pay me, I do it for what it costs. When they can't pay, I do it for them anyway. Knowing the kids need it is enough compensation for me."

The fat man looked at McGregor. The boy had stopped eating, and three of the sandwiches were gone. He turned away again. "My work takes me all over the West. I'm due in a little town south of Phoenix by noon tomorrow."

"*Phoenix?*" For the first time McGregor showed interest.

"Yes, Phoenix," the fat man said, chuckling. "Oh, I'll be there on time, all right. Lots of speed in this sweet baby." His hands patted the wheel. "She's marvelous on the flats, mountains, twists, turns, anything. They're all the same to her. We'll be leaving Utah in a couple of hours now."

"Utah?" Again McGregor disclosed interest.

"Yes, Utah." The man turned his eyes away from the road and caught McGregor's gaze. Again he saw that look, and this time he was certain it was a hunted look. The kid was afraid, and running from something. He had seen that look in others. He didn't like it. He was getting uneasy again.

Focusing on the road, he said, "But maybe you don't want to go as far as Arizona. Maybe you'll be getting out before?"

Once more came the hesitant voice. "No." There was a long pause, and then, "I—I'll go to Arizona."

"You mean all the way to Phoenix?"

"Ye-s, all the way to . . ." The voice went on but it was too low and the words too incoherent for the man to understand.

Pudgy fingers tightened about the wheel. The fat man was conscious of fear mounting within him. Had he gotten into more than he'd bargained for? He'd come close to it once or twice before in picking up the wrong kind. But it was worse now with only mountains and desert country ahead, for to save time he had picked a road that was little used. The night would be a long one. He felt the weight of the revolver in his pocket. At least he could count on that for help, if he needed it.

An hour passed, and then another. The fat man kept talking, as much to keep himself wide awake as to endure his fear. But McGregor never said a word. The kid's eyes were closed yet he wasn't sleeping, his breathing was not regular enough for that. The man told himself he was only exaggerating his situation. There was nothing to fear. McGregor might be running from something, but he was unarmed and only a boy. Yet his body was lean and lithe and powerful, that of a born athlete. It was then that the man decided he would not pull up to the side of the road for an hour's sleep, as was his usual custom, before going on.

For several more hours he skillfully guided the plunging, powerful car through mountainous country. He was well into Arizona when his eyes became so heavy that he was hardly able to hold them open. If he had been alone, he would have stopped, for it was time to rest a while.

The clock said almost one o'clock. He turned on the radio, hoping the loud dance music would keep him awake and alert. McGregor stirred. Glancing at him, the fat man saw the kid's hand go to his pocket. He saw the bulge. McGregor had his hand on something! A gun? Could the kid have a gun there? He reached for his own. "What are you doing, McGregor? What do you have in your pocket?"

The boy's eyes were furtive. "N-nothing," he said.

"Play square with me," the fat man said. "If I hadn't picked you up . . ." The music blared, drowning out his words, and then became softer. "You pull a gun on me, and I'll put this car into that ravine. It'll be the end of both of us."

"No gun," the boy said. He held the dark-stained money in his hand for the fat man to see.

The big shoulders relaxed behind the wheel. The man turned his eyes away. "That's a lot of money." He said just that, and nothing more. Where the kid had gotten it was none of his business. "Stay out of this," he told himself. *"Get rid of him as soon as you can."*

He concentrated on his driving. He took the car down the last mountainside with the rush of a toboggan. Going across a great open stretch of land, he stepped even harder upon the accelerator. He turned up the radio. Another hour passed and his heavy lids began dropping again in spite of all he could do. Finally he knew he had to close his eyes, if only for a few minutes. It was either that or fall asleep behind the wheel.

Slowing the car, he said, "My eyes are tired. I'm going to rest them for a few minutes." He didn't know if the boy heard him. It didn't matter. He had to stop, and he had a gun to protect himself.

He kept the rear wheels of the convertible on the road. He had passed through this desert wasteland before, and knew what it meant to get his car stuck in the sand. He wanted none of that tonight. He turned off the engine, but not the radio. He wouldn't sleep. He'd just close his eyes, rest them for a little while.

The music stopped and the announcer gave the time. Two o'clock. He adjusted the clock on the dashboard. The kid was still huddled in the corner, his eyes closed. He shut his own eyes. A moment passed, another. Or was it an hour? Was he dreaming or did he hear a voice saying, *". . . south of Salt Lake City. The three men were captured an hour after the daring theft, but the boy who accompanied them escaped the police. Also missing is the money, two hundred dollars, taken from the diner's cash-*

ier. The boy is believed to have the money. His description is: Between sixteen and eighteen years of age, about five feet five inches, red hair, and lightly built. He was injured during the fight that took place in the diner. He'll have cuts and abrasions on face and body. The Utah state police . . ."

The fat man opened his eyes. He turned, to find the boy listening and staring at him. "Get out," the man said. "Stay outside the car until I'm ready to go. I can't trust you now that I know what you're running from."

When the man was alone he locked the doors, telling himself that he didn't know anything for certain. The boy might not be the same one they were looking for, even though the description fitted, the money fitted. He was just being careful. There was no sense taking any chances. The kid might lift his gun, that is, if it *was* the same kid. As long as he didn't get hurt himself, this was none of his business. Turning kids over to the police wasn't for him. Besides, he was a long way from Salt Lake City and Utah. He didn't want to do anything that would keep him from his work, his work helping young people . . .

The fat man went to sleep, thus missing still another news announcement that had to do with another boy . . . *"the search through northwestern Wyoming for Alec Ramsay and his famous black horse is still going on. Even now, during this, the second night, planes are circling above the ranges, their pilots watching for a light, a signal from Alec Ramsay to indicate that he's still alive. But experienced woodsmen are pessimistic over the chances of the boy's safety. They say the possibility of his survival in that desolate country is slight. However, Alec Ramsay's father and his close friend, the well-known trainer Henry Dailey, refuse to believe this. Mr. Dailey said only an hour ago, 'Alec is not dead. If he was I'd feel it. A part of me would have died with him, and I'd know. That hasn't happened. He's alive. Somewhere out there he's alive and waiting for us to find him.'"*

The fat man snored through it all. When he awakened, his eyes were rested, and he was ready to go on. Opening the far door, he said, "Get in now, McGregor. I'll drop you off at the next town. What you may have done is none of my business."

From outside came only silence, the utter silence of desert wastes. He moved over to the window, and could see nothing in the blackness. He got a flashlight, and went outside. But he could not find the boy. "McGregor!" he shouted. "McGregor!" But only the far-off barking of a coyote answered his calls. He got back in the car, and turned the ignition key. The engine roared, but still he didn't put the car in gear. He felt guilty about leaving the kid behind. He opened the door again to shout into the night, and then he closed it hard.

He put the car in gear, and started moving. Why should he feel guilty? he asked himself. No reason at all. Actually he was giving the kid a break. He wasn't turning him over to the police, was he? And he could have done that. No, instead he was forgetting about this whole business. No one would ever hear anything about Mc-Gregor from him. He was helping the kid along. He was giving him a break. He was always interested in helping

THE LONG NIGHT   83

kids, helping young people. Wasn't that what he always said?

The low and powerful convertible rushed across the great desert with more speed than ever before. It seemed that the fat man who guided it was running away from something, too, even as his thoughts ran on: *Poor kid on the lam. McGregor had picked the wrong time to leave. He should have waited a few more hours. There's nothing out there where he's going . . . only sand. The poor, thieving kid.*

Strange Awakening

7

He stumbled often, yet his eyes never left the long black mountain range rising ahead of him. There he would find seclusion and peace. Soon, he thought, he would come to it, not knowing that the haven that seemed so near was fifty miles away. He realized he was in desert country by the feel of the sand on his bare feet, and beneath his hands when he fell.

For the first hour the going wasn't hard. The long car ride had fortified him and, although his head still throbbed, he felt none of the stabbing pains. Nor did he feel any of the loneliness that comes with such vast stretches of desert wastes, nor any of the hopelessness. He was free of the fat man who would have turned him over to the police. The sand was cold and comforting on his feet. The wind was cutting yet somehow it, too, comforted him. From far away came the deep mournful howl of a wolf on the hunt, yet he did not hear it. He was running away, and his ears were closed to everything but the sound of his own steps as he put more distance between himself and those who would pursue him.

Sometime during the long hours that followed, his head pains returned. It was then that he began crawling, sometimes on hands and knees but most often on his stomach, wriggling like a snake. Yet he kept going, believing he would soon reach the mountains, and knowing that this night had to come to an end, that it could not last forever.

He was conscious of the coming of morning. The air was clear and cold, but a redness showed from behind the walls of the eastern peaks, a redness that was growing brighter and brighter. For a moment he forgot his pain and agony to watch the rising of the sun. He had lived in a world of darkness for so long. Now that it had ended he might be able to remember all that had happened to him before it began.

The sun mounted, and he felt its early warmth. It gave him new hope and encouragement to go on in spite of his pain. He staggered to his feet, only to find that the mountains were no closer than they had been during the night. But soon, soon he would reach them. The sun's ruddiness had transformed his world into one of red earth with bared, golden rock exposed here and there to break up its flatness. Not far ahead he could see rolling terraces, even low hills, of purples and yellows. But the reds were there, too, the blood-reds of the desert.

Beyond all these were the mountains, their profiles clear and distinct in the early morning light. He stumbled forward, determined in spite of his pain to stay on his feet, to reach the mountains before another night fell.

The sun climbed higher, and with its ascent the desert changed. The air close to the earth moved, shifted, and finally began a dance of many colors. The boy raised the back of his hands frequently to wipe away great drops of sweat from his face. No longer could he see the mountains, only the dancing veils of purples and pinks and yellows above the blood-reds.

The desert was now showing itself to him for what it was, a deadly land of intolerable heat, a land set apart from the rest of the world, and to be looked upon curiously from a safe distance. He wanted to turn and run, but he could do neither. His body seemed to be aflame with the great waves of heat that enveloped him. He felt no other pain but that which came from this inferno. He lost all track of time, not knowing if he crawled or lay still, and not caring.

A feeling of great peace and languor swept over him. The desert became hazy, nothing real, nothing important. He felt blissfully happy and very, very sleepy. He tried to raise one hand to his face, but he couldn't move it. His hand was too heavy, too big. The whole world was growing heavier, bigger. He let his head rest on the earth, that blood-red earth. "Soon I'll sleep," he said, "very soon now, then everything will be all right."

There was no beginning or end to his sleep. But at some point during this indefinite period he felt hands upon him again. *Always hands.* Was he never to be free of them? Would they never leave him alone? Then he felt something cool and wet in his mouth, flowing down his throat, quenching the fires burning within him. His thick lips moved, and he mumbled, "My name is McGregor."

At another point during this period he felt strong arms lifting him, carrying him. He didn't care, and slipped back quickly into his oblivion. At still another time he felt a movement beneath him, and his head seemed to be resting against skin, a skin covered with coarse hair. But this held no interest for him, either.

There were other periods, many of them, some coming in quick succession, and others at long intervals. The flickering of a fire . . . a glow in the dark . . . squinting eyes and then blackness engulfing him once more. The hands coming again . . . the hands *always* . . . holding his head, and bringing wetness and comfort, lifting him, carrying him to the coarse hair. Again movement, periods of never-ending movement, periods of silence and stillness.

Toward the end of his oblivion, he became aware of the hoofed feet beneath him and knew he was being carried by an animal. He tried lifting his head from the bobbing neck, but hands from the side gently restrained him.

"Stay down," a voice said.

It was easy to do as he was told. He knew he did not have the strength to raise his head. He sank back into his darkness, remembering only that the voice had been soft, and the hands gentle.

It was night when he opened his eyes again. He saw the

flaring of the fire from where he lay and then, coming within its brightness, a man's silhouette. "My name is McGregor," he said.

The voice, the gentle voice, came out of the night. "I know it is. You've told me so many times."

He felt the spoon between his teeth. He felt the warmth of the liquid flowing down his throat. He opened his mouth for more and more, and he was not disappointed. Finally he heard the voice again. "Go to sleep now. We'll be traveling again in a little while."

He did as he was told, and soon he felt the hands go about him, carrying him to the animal. Once more they began moving.

When next he opened his eyes, it was late morning. Ahead were the mountains, boldly defined, but still in the distance. He knew he was in the foothills, that the desert had been left behind. He knew it by the gentle ascent of the land, and the scattered oak trees. He knew it by the small yet frequent currents of cool air that penetrated the clinging furnace-like heat of the desert. He knew it by the sweet smells of the pine trees brought down by these air currents from the high country. He felt hope and life stir within him. The foothills did this for him, the foothills together with the kind hands and voice at his side.

He was aware of many things that day. He learned it was a burro he rode. He knew this by the long ears that flopped just above his head. He learned, too, that the man walked close beside him but a little to the rear, steadying his body to keep it on the burro's back. He could not see him.

For hours the trail wound upward. The hills grew bigger and the trees more numerous. The sun was warm and drowsy, but no longer hot. The air became sharp and clear. Above, and still far away, were the mountains, their hard sharp surfaces brilliant beneath a cloudless sky. The boy looked upon all this until he could hold his eyes open no longer, and then slept.

When he awakened, they were in the high pines. The ground was no longer covered with brown brush but with emerald-green grass. They crossed a small open meadow that swept up to the deep refreshing shadows of the pines. They entered the woods again, and the trail became one of velvet needles that muffled the sound of the burro's hoofs and the man's feet. They continued ever upward, sometimes passing through more open meadows and valleys but mostly through the long aisles of the great pines.

He was half-asleep, half-awake during the rest of the afternoon. He was conscious always of the sweet smell of the tall trees, and the wind that played like a great organ through their tops. The air was cold, and it seemed that he would never get enough of it.

It was almost sunset when they came to another open meadow, no larger or smaller than many they had left behind them. In the center was a cottage. Large patches of brilliantly colored flowers grew behind the picket fence that encircled it. As they neared the cottage, the cold air carried the perfumed scents of the flowers to the boy. They crossed a shallow, rushing brook, and down in the shadows of the trees a startled deer stopped drinking.

He raised his head to look at them, then bounded away into the woods.

They came to a stop before the fence, and the gentle voice said, "We're home now."

Strong arms lifted him off the burro's back, and he tried to tell this man that he needn't be carried, that he would walk. But he found he could not move his tongue to form the words, and the effort only served to make his head throb again. He was carried into the cottage, his lips moving but making no sound. He was placed down on something, and by its softness he knew it had to be a bed. He felt the man's hands again as the blankets were pulled over him. Once more the voice came. "Go to sleep now. It's been long and hard. You'll feel . . ."

He went to sleep, the first peaceful sleep he had ever known.

The night passed, and then came another day. Another night, another day. He was well aware now of the passing of time. He knew the days by the bright sun coming through the white-curtained window at the foot of his bed. He knew the nights. They never held total blackness any more. Always a lamp burned in the other room. Beneath it he sometimes saw the man. He knew him now, knew that his hands were not only kind but long-fingered and deeply tanned, like his face. The man was very tall and leanly built, and his eyes, beneath bushy sun-whitened brows, were keen and clear.

The morning finally came when he realized he was getting well. He awakened to find that his head no longer throbbed and that the swelling was down. But it was still sensitive to his touch so he let it alone. Finally he formed words with his lips, and then tried whispering to himself. His sentences came forth the way he wanted them said, coherent and understandable.

He looked around the room, actually seeing it for the first time. He noticed the clean, white curtains hung on every window, the deep-red carpet on the floor, the chairs of many brilliant colors, and the dresser with its tidy cloth. He saw the hairbrush and comb, the shaving cream and lotions, all neatly placed on the dresser. Beyond, in the open closet, were flannel shirts and worn leather jackets, wide-rimmed sombreros, and stout high-laced boots. Hanging high on the back wall were many ropes and rifles.

The clothing and the equipment belonged to a man who, with his burro, traveled in ever-changing altitudes . . . through hot, arid foothills and the desert, through the cold of the high country. Somehow they did not go with this room, this clean, orderly room of clashing, brilliant colors.

The door opened and the man stood there. "How do you feel this morning? Better?"

"Yes, better. I think I'm all right."

"Fine! I was figuring on that. I have a good breakfast ready for you. It'll really fix you up."

The man left, yet his voice stayed in the room. It was a low, cultured voice. It belonged to this orderly room, and not to a desert wanderer. He had been wearing a white shirt and tie, well-pressed pants, and soft slippers. Was this the man who had walked endless miles beside him under the hot sun of the desert?

The man returned, carrying a breakfast tray which he

placed on the bedside table. He propped pillows behind the boy, and then transferred the tray to the bed. Two fried eggs, crisp bacon, toast and jelly. "Go ahead and eat," he said. "I guess you can do it without my help this morning." He smiled. It was a warm, good smile, disclosing even, white teeth. He looked younger than he was, closer to forty than to sixty, which was probably his real age. "Eggs from my own chickens," he said, "laid fresh this morning for you." He pulled up a chair to the bed, his eyes resting a moment on the yellow fabric that covered the chair's straight back. "What color is this, anyway?" he asked suddenly.

"Color? I—it's yellow."

The man laughed. "I bought it for a brown one. That's what they told me it was at the store. I'm color-blind. Blind as a bat to colors." He met the boy's eyes. "Go ahead and eat, McGregor. I'll keep quiet for a while, if my talking bothers you. But you see, I don't have many guests. Maybe just two or three in the six years I've been here." He paused. "And I forgot to ask my other guests about the color of these chairs."

"But how do you know my name is McGregor?"

"You must have told me so at least a hundred times during the past week." The tall man smiled. "Mine's Gordon."

"I've been with you a week?"

"Yes, a week since we picked you up."

"*We?*"

"Goldie and I," the man said. "Goldie's my burro, my pal." He paused, the tiny creases at the corners of his clear eyes crinkling again. "His full name is Black

Gold. I named him after the 1924 winner of the Kentucky Derby.''

Black Gold. Kentucky Derby. The boy felt his mind groping, trying to respond to these names. He shut his eyes, hoping to help himself, hoping to overcome the mental barrier that would not permit his memory to return. His face whitened at his great effort, and then suddenly saddened. He knew he was beaten, that it was still too early, that it would take time, perhaps a long time, before he'd be able to remember anything. He opened his eyes and met the man's gaze.

"Does your head still hurt?" Gordon asked.

"No . . . it isn't that."

"Then you're worrying more about what you don't know is true," Gordon said. "You forget all that, Mc-Gregor, and you'll get well a lot faster."

The boy's eyes were alive with fear. He wanted to run again. "I—I don't know what you mean," he said.

Gordon rose to his feet, standing tall and lean above the bed. "You told me everything in your delirium," he said quietly. "You think the Utah state police are after you. You think you're wanted by them for robbery, and you're running away. Maybe they are after you. I don't know. But then *you* don't know for certain, either. You've been hurt so you can't remember anything . . . *even your name.* You said you assumed the name Mc-Gregor. So, I wouldn't jump to any conclusions now, if I were you. There'll be time enough for all that later. Just figure on getting well. After that, you can make your own decision about what to do."

He walked over to the high dresser and, opening the

top right-hand drawer, removed an envelope. Inside was the bloodstained money. "It's all here," he said. "Let it stay here, and forget about it until you're well. If you know then it's not yours, you can decide for yourself the right thing to do. But don't convict yourself before you know for certain you've committed a crime. Your big job is to get well, and living with a guilt complex won't help you do it."

He went to the door. "And don't worry so much about assuming another name, McGregor," he said. "Names don't mean anything in this country. One's as good as another. Keep McGregor. It's a good one. So is Gordon . . . and that's not my right name, either." Smiling, he closed the door behind him, leaving the boy alone.

The Pines

8

During the week that followed, the boy learned all he needed to know about Gordon. Actually the man's *first* name was Gordon; his last name was Davis. But he had not used the latter in the six years he had been living in the pine country. There was no sinister reason for the omission. Gordon simply wanted to break away completely from the old life and habits of one Gordon Davis.

He had talked a great deal that week, as though most happy to have a guest in his home.

"A few years ago I wouldn't have told this to anyone. I didn't even think about it," he said. "I wanted nothing to remind me of Hollywood. I hated the sound of my own name. I more than hated it. I was afraid of it. *Gordon Davis,* managing editor of that slick, pseudo-glamour movie magazine *Seeing Stars*! I can say it now, and it

95

doesn't bother me at all. I know that life's all over for me. But what the devil, the name Gordon alone is good enough." He laughed. "In fact, I don't even need that much. It doesn't matter around here. Over at the general store in Leesburg they call me 'Slim, the Burro Man.' That's enough identification for anyone around these parts.

"I went to work on *Seeing Stars* at the age of fourteen, and thirty years later became editor. I spent ten more years in that job before chucking the whole thing. I was sick of the business, sick of Hollywood, sick of the world. I guess I'd felt that way for years, but never had the gumption to do anything about it. One day my secretary hands me a deed to an acre of land. 'Look,' she says, 'what the publicity department of that movie epic *Sea of Pines* has come up with. They've given you an acre of pine woodland in Arizona!'

"Well, sure enough, that's exactly what those guys had done to publicize their forthcoming picture," Gordon continued. "And there's no telling how many newspaper and magazine editors in the country got deeds like mine." He smiled. "But I think I'm the only one who paid my taxes on the property, and then finally moved off to live on it. I've never had a moment's regret. Oh, it wasn't easy at first, but before long I had it like I wanted it. So now I'm happy and set in my ways just like any old city bachelor, only I'm up here in the pines and alone. I like being alone. I'll always like it after what I've gone through in Hollywood. I've got a town, this Leesburg, just over the mountain range. It's close enough, twenty-one miles through the Cut. I get to town maybe once a month for supplies, less often if I can manage it.

"The rest of the time I spend right around here, taking care of myself, the house, old Goldie and my flowers. I guess you're kind of surprised at my having so many flowers, now that you know I'm color-blind. But there's nothing wrong with my nose. I can still smell. And that makes up for my not being able to appreciate their beauty.

"Of course I'm away a lot, too. Goldie and I know our way around most of these woods, the mountains and the desert country. We go out prospecting for gold and silver."

Gordon's clear eyes were always bright when he spoke of his journeys. "I'm no hermit, but a prospector. Think of me as that, McGregor." And then he would go on, spending hours telling of his far wanderings through high and low country, searching for his elusive strike. "There was a time in a deep canyon I call the Gory Rut that . . . And another time over beyond the Red Monument . . . Then back a few years ago I spent a month on Buckskin Ridge and there . . . But you can't ignore the desert so let me tell you about the time . . ."

For most of the week the boy listened to Gordon tell in detail of his years on the trail with Goldie. He listened, and forgot for a while his own problems in the story of the man's quest for gold and silver. But at last he came to realize that Gordon actually cared nothing at all about acquiring new wealth. His interest was in the constant search that took him away even from the simple comforts he had here in his meadow home, an endless search that led through canyons, gorges and valleys, across waste-lands, woods and ridges. All these mysterious, untouched lands Gordon loved. He was eager to see them with his own eyes, and then to look at what lay beyond.

But the following week Gordon spoke little of himself, his journeys or his life in the pines. It was as if he had talked his fill, and now wanted to be left alone again. Once he even forgot why the boy was there, for he said, "Your face is familiar, McGregor. Have you ever been in Hollywood?" Not until he saw the whiteness come to the boy's face did he remember. Not until he heard him say *"I don't know"* did he mumble an abrupt apology for his own forgetfulness, and go outside to tend to his flowers.

It was during this week that the boy was most misera-ble. His body had regained its strength and he felt completely well except for the headaches that came perhaps once or twice a day to remind him of his injury. But he lived with the bitter torment that while his physical condition had improved considerably his mind hadn't. There was no sign of mental recovery, nothing that encouraged him to think, to hope that in time his memory would return.

Conscious of the boy's mental agony, Gordon tried to do everything he could to help him. He talked a little more during the week that followed. Again he veered from the set pattern of his bachelor life to make the boy more comfortable. He offered him his bed again instead of the living-room couch. But the boy refused. Gordon told him every night to use the big leather chair in the living room, and to feel free to read any of his books. But always the boy refused, saying that he was all right, that he didn't want to get in the way at all, and that he appreciated everything Gordon had done for him.

So Gordon resigned himself to helping the boy in the only way left. He spent longer hours in the kitchen, cooking the most nourishing meals he knew . . . stewed young chicken with hot broth and potatoes and green vegetables, roast lamb and beef and salads . . . meals such as one would get only in fine restaurants and good homes. He set these dishes down on clean tablecloths, urging the boy to eat everything before him.

One night he said, "You must face the fact that you've suffered a head concussion, and that's been followed by amnesia. I suppose it's only because you were in fine physical shape that you were able to get along without medical attention. Now you're on the way to complete recovery. But to make it come even faster you've got to have plenty of rest and nourishment. That's all any doctor would tell you, I'm sure."

"What good is my being physically well, *if I can't remember?"* McGregor asked bitterly.

"Your memory will come back, too, if you're healthy and want it back."

"Want it back?" A thin smile crept on the boy's face. *"Don't you think I do?"*

The man looked at McGregor a long while, and then said, "Yes . . . yes, I guess you do, at that." He turned away guiltily. "The last few days I got to thinking that maybe you didn't want to regain your memory," he admitted. "I've heard of some people creating a mental block because they don't want to remember their past." He met the boy's eyes again, those tragic, saddened eyes. "I was wrong," he said.

"You were thinking of the money in the dresser," McGregor said accusingly. "You thought that since the police are after me . . ." He paused. "I want to remember everything," he began again, heatedly. "I don't care what happens to me after that. I can face it then. You've got to believe that."

"I believe you, and if you want your memory back it'll come."

"But how? What good is my wanting it back, if the barrier is always there?"

"It's half the job," the man said. "The other half is complete physical recovery from your injury."

The boy smiled bitterly. "Then I should be completely well," he said. "I feel fine."

"No, it isn't that fast. You have to work for it. There are steps you must take."

"Steps?"

"Yes, steps. Your body, your hands must have been trained to do something. Start using them, and maybe you'll find out what it was. Something you do should come easier, more natural to you than anything else. Pursue whatever that is, and perhaps the association of this and what comes from it will make something else more familiar. Follow that line and somewhere along it you should get your memory back."

Gordon left the room. He returned a moment later,

carrying a rifle which he handed to the boy. "Let's see you hold it, feel it," he said abruptly.

The boy's hands slid down the long barrel. The rifle was light in his hands but there was nothing familiar about it. Instead he lifted it awkwardly to his shoulder.

Seeing this, Gordon quickly took the rifle away from him. "You sure never handled a rifle much," he said. Then he pushed something else into the boy's hand, his eyes intent, watching every move.

The boy looked down at the small revolver, and was afraid to close his fingers about it. He was afraid because of what he might learn. But finally he made himself grasp it. He felt the polished butt in the palm of his right hand, the trigger beneath his finger. He raised it, sighting it.

"You've closed the wrong eye," Gordon said. "Keep them both open or just close the left one." Then he took back the revolver, making no effort to conceal his relief at the boy's being no more familiar with the revolver than with the rifle. He smiled. "Whatever you've done hasn't been in this line," he said. "That's good to know."

The days that followed were easier for McGregor. He had some kind of plan now, and it was far better than just sitting around the house, waiting for the black mental curtain to rise.

He worked with the flowers and plants, cutting them back and planting new ones. He spaded the earth, and rubbed the dirt in his hands, hoping that just the feel of it would awaken some remembrance of similar activity. He brought the dirt close to his nose, smelling it as he did the flowers. But the moist earth, the perfume-scented flowers did nothing for him, awakened nothing.

His nights were spent reading the many books in Gordon's library, hoping that some page, perhaps just a single sentence would provide him with a key that would open other doors now so securely locked.

One afternoon, thinking the fishing rod he held in his hands felt a little familiar, he went to the meadow stream. Walking along, he found a black pool where fish swarmed in the depths. He found himself shortening his line, and somehow the leader and the fly seemed familiar, too. He must have fished before, and within him rose a keen sense of anticipation, of frenzied hope. Maybe here was his key! He slid down the steep grassy bank, and then stopped. He drew his arm back, his wrist snapped. The reel whirled beneath his thumb. He had cast easily. He had fished before! There was no doubt of it! The fly rested but a second on the surface of the stream, and then came a flash of a white body from the deep blackness. He felt the fish strike, but he was hardly conscious of the fight to land it.

Later he held his catch in his hands, looking at it as if he expected the fish to speak and tell him who he really was. He sat there until the stream became dark in the deep shadows of the setting sun. Finally he got to his feet, and started back for the cottage. He had found something he had done before. He had found a key *but it had opened no other doors*. A feeling of bitterness, of utter defeat and hopelessness walked with him. Nothing would change, ever change, for him.

The next few days he did nothing. Gordon watched him

and offered no sympathy. "This is your fight, Mc-Gregor," the man said. "No one can help you but yourself." The boy remained silent.

Early the following week Gordon said, "I'm going to town for supplies. You can come or stay here just as you like." He didn't meet the boy's eyes.

McGregor knew it was time to go, that Gordon had had enough of playing host and friend and nursemaid to him. Gordon wanted to be left alone, to live the quiet, secluded life he had chosen for himself six years ago.

"I'll go with you," he said.

Surprised, the man looked up. "It's an all-day trip," he said, "and you'll have to walk. Goldie will be carrying some books I'm mailing back to a friend in California."

McGregor carried his breakfast dishes to the sink. "I've walked before," he said, and then his eyes dropped to the high boots he wore. "I'll have to keep these," he added, "and your clothes. But some day . . ."

"You're coming back with me. You're welcome here."

The boy washed the dishes. "No, you've done enough. As you said the other night, it's my fight. No one can help me but myself."

"I didn't mean it the way it must have sounded to you, McGregor."

"It sounded all right. It still makes sense. I'll find a way out."

"There's not much to do in Leesburg. It's pretty small."

"Then I'll go on until I find work."

"You got that money to help . . ." Gordon stopped

abruptly when the boy turned and faced him.

"Keep it," McGregor said. "I don't even want to think about it now. Later, when I learn . . ."

The tall man stood up. "All right, if you want it that way. It'll be here when you decide what to do with it." He went to the sink, and together they finished the dishes in silence.

Goldie stood still, awaiting his pack. Gordon fondled the burro's head, but his eyes were inquisitively watching the boy. McGregor had gone for the hobbled burro at the far end of the meadow. He had taken the halter and put it on Goldie *before* taking off the burro's hobbles.

"Perhaps," Gordon thought, "I'm putting too much emphasis on this. But remember my first time with Goldie? Tenderfoot that I was, I went and freed Goldie of his hobbles, and *then* tried to get the halter on him. I chased him for an hour, and never would have caught him without help."

He watched McGregor run the currycomb and brush over Goldie, cleaning the burro's long hair until it shone in the sun. And then the kid took the saddle blankets, placing them carefully upon Goldie's back, making certain they were smoothly folded so there would be no chafing. Next came the pack saddle. Gordon hung back, helping only a little, his eyes never leaving the boy's hands. The kid was just as careful with the saddle as he had been with the blankets. McGregor got it in place and then buckled the girth straps, not too tight, not too loose. His hands moved quickly, surely. The kid had saddled before, and often. There could be no doubt of this. Yet

McGregor wasn't even aware of what his hands were telling him. He was too busy at his job.

Only when the pack itself was placed on Goldie's back did the boy hesitate and fumble. Gordon went to work then, drawing the pack ropes tight and fastening the boxes firmly so they wouldn't slip. "Nothing is worse than a loose hitch," he said. "If the pack slides or comes apart, Goldie will take off, and we'll be all day trailing him and picking up the books from the mountainside." His hands moved expertly, and his eyes were bright with his pride in a packer's art. For a while he forgot the boy who was watching him.

They were well on their way through the pines when Gordon got to thinking again of McGregor's skill in handling and saddling Goldie. Yet he hesitated to mention it. The kid had learned he had fished before, but it hadn't helped. In fact, it had made things worse. McGregor expected too much too fast. So Gordon decided to say nothing about it.

More than an hour later, the boy said, "I've been thinking about Goldie's name. I mean his full name, *Black Gold*."

Gordon didn't turn back to look at him. "Why? What's wrong with it?"

"There's nothing wrong with it. You say Black Gold won the Kentucky Derby?"

"Yes, back in 1924."

The boy remained silent for a long while so Gordon spoke again. "I guess I didn't tell you that I'm interested in the thoroughbred. Or at least I was before coming here. Don't have much chance to follow the breed now.''

"The thoroughbred?"

"Yes, that's what I said . . . the race horse, the horse that's been bred to race for centuries, not the quarter horse they have in this state that they're trying to make into a race horse. Luckily, I don't see much of people around here. The way I feel about the thoroughbred and they feel about their quarter horse only makes for an argument. Oh, don't get me wrong, there's nothing wrong with their horses, if they use them for what they've been developed to do, and don't make unjustified claims as to their racing ability. Sure, they're fast up to a quarter of a mile, and once in a while a furlong farther. They're handy and quick and easy to handle. They're the ideal *working cow horse.* The best of them do have some thoroughbred or standardbred or Morgan blood in them, if you trace back their bloodlines. But to hear some of the folks talk in Leesburg, the quarter horse is a *breed* of long standing. He isn't at all, he's a *type* of horse that's been developed to work the range. He's no race horse.''

The boy spoke, his voice hesitant as if he were a little unsure of himself. "You can't blame people for loving any kind of a race, no matter how long or how short, and for loving their horses regardless of type or breed.''

Gordon turned, his eyes studying the boy's face. He remembered again McGregor's hands as he had saddled Goldie, and now the kid had spoken of people's love for racing with an understanding that couldn't be ignored. No doubt about it, the kid had had something to do with horses at one time or another. And come to think of it, he had the build of a born rider. Gordon turned again to the trail ahead, but his eyes lost none of their thoughtfulness. Sometime, somewhere, he'd seen this kid. Where? Anything to do with horses? Couldn't be. He'd been here for six years, and the few horses he'd seen were the cow horses in Leesburg. It wasn't there. He was certain of that. And there was no sense in thinking back six years to the California tracks, for the kid was too young for that. How about the magazines? How about the issues of *Thoroughbred Record* that Lew Miller had sent him a year ago, and which he'd read and returned? Could he have seen a picture of the kid in one of them?

Finally he said, "I'll bet you'll find you like horses, McGregor."

"I like Goldie, anyway," the boy replied.

They crossed a meadow, and then the trail descended into a long valley. They were nearing the mountain range.

"Maybe you can get a job near Leesburg," Gordon said thoughtfully. "There's a man named Allen you might get along with pretty well. He's an Easterner and brought some friends along with him to settle down here. Three years ago it was, and he and his pals have been playing cowboy ever since." He laughed. "But I guess I can't criticize them too much for that. For six years I've been playing prospector. Anyway, this fellow Allen had the money to buy up the best water and grazing land in the Leesburg area. He's got cattle and quarter horses. Just now he's more interested in the horses. He's got the three-year-old champ at three hundred yards . . . won with him last year. Since then he's been walking around town like he owned Satan."

"Satan?"

Gordon turned at the sudden intensity of the boy's voice. He saw the white face, skin drawn tight, and the eyes that reflected conflicting emotions. An awareness of something familiar was there at first, then came a groping, a groping for identity. Finally the eyes were filled with deep sadness as the boy lost his mental fight.

Gordon spoke softly. "Satan is a race horse," he said, "a champion in his day."

"I know," the boy said. "Somehow I know. *But why?*" He put a hand to his head.

"You got your headache back?"

"Just a little. It'll go away."

"We'll take a rest before we go through the Cut," Gordon said. "It'll make it easier for you."

He decided to speak no more about horses. But when he got to town he'd drop a line to Lew Miller, asking him to send another batch of the *Thoroughbred Record* for him to read. Maybe he'd find something in them that would give him a clue to the boy's identity. But what about the bloodstained money back at the cottage? What good would it do to be able to tell the boy who he was, if it meant that he was wanted by the police for the Utah robbery? And what good would it do him? He wouldn't rest very easy, knowing for certain that he had harbored a fugitive, that he had known his whereabouts all along without telling the authorities. Perhaps it would be best to stay out of this altogether from now on. Just try to get the kid a job at the Allen ranch, and then go home and take up where he'd left off before the boy came. It was the easiest way.

So, with McGregor following him, Gordon led his burro down the long valley at the foot of the mountains. He did not know, because he had no radio, of the futile search still going on in northern Wyoming for Alec Ramsay, who had ridden Satan in some of his greatest triumphs. A heartbreaking search that now had been forsaken by all save a small, private land party organized by Henry Dailey, who refused to give up because *"Alec is not dead. If he was I'd feel it. A part of me would be gone, would have died with him, and I'd know. . . ."*

And far from Wyoming, too, grazed a tall black stallion, the sire of Satan. He wasn't the Black of four weeks ago. Now his fine mane and tail were matted and heavy with burrs, brush, and pine needles. His unshod hoofs were worn and hard from running at top speed over rocks, boulders and sagebrush. He had learned to run lightly, making scarcely a sound no matter what the terrain might be. His great body was torn and scarred from the rakings of savage teeth and claws. Yet he had survived his terrible battles, and now, shining in his eyes, was the wild look of an animal who knew desolate country, and feared neither it nor man nor beast. His body was thin yet hard from spending weeks on the short forage of the high mountain country. In spite of his ragged appearance, his wind and endurance were of the best.

Now he stopped grazing to sniff the wind. Then he whistled, and started his band traveling again. The mares moved at his command . . . the sorrels, bays, piebalds, buckskins and palominos. Some of them were wild mustangs who had never known the touch of man, others wore the brands of ranches in Wyoming, Utah and Arizona. They were less than a hundred miles from where Gordon and the boy called McGregor stopped to rest before entering the mountain pass that would take them to Leesburg.

Horse Trader

9

Gordon spoke no more about horses. He had dropped the subject, and did not mean to bring it up again. Nor was the boy anxious to pursue it. The long hike had brought back his headache, and he wanted only to rest, hoping to get rid of his pain again.

For half an hour they sat before the Cut, and then McGregor got to his feet. "I'm ready if you are," he said.

"Headache gone?"

McGregor nodded. Gordon rose, taking hold of his burro. He didn't need to tell the kid that the roughest part of the trip was still ahead of them. McGregor could see that for himself. For five more hours the trail would be back-breaking but safe. They would climb two thousand feet, and then drop four thousand. There would probably be a bear or two to contend with somewhere on the trail,

111

for the Cut was the easiest pass across this range, and bears were the most skilled of all animals in finding the least difficult route. Gordon held his rifle ready.

They went slowly up the steep ascent, stopping every half-hour to rest a few minutes before going on again. They were hemmed in by cliffs thousands of feet high. The air became thinner, and their breathing more labored. They saw a bear feeding and Gordon used his rifle at a distance of three hundred yards and missed. From then on they were constantly on the lookout for the bear, but he never reappeared. As they continued climbing, the very tops of the cliffs came down to meet them, and soon they seemed close beneath the sky.

They rested again at the summit of the Cut. They sat on rocks with tumultuous boulders and slabs of sheer stone all around them. But above and beyond rose the giant peaks, calm and stately in the peaceful stillness of the upper air.

They didn't speak. Gordon only nodded toward the drop in the trail ahead of them, and the boy understood. From now on they'd be going down. The worst was behind them. They sat for a long while in the mountain silence. There was a wind but it passed over bare rock and made no noise. It could move nothing up here.

Finally they began their descent. The trail was steep, and all their efforts now were bent in holding themselves back from going too fast and slipping on the loose shale beneath their feet. Once more the walls of the high crevice closed in about them, shutting out the sky except for a narrow strip of light at the very top. For three more hours the trail continued to be steep, hard and long, and then with startling abruptness the crevice came to an end. They emerged upon a bright sunlit plateau. Far in the distance, and across this broad strip of flat, open land, were other ranges. Mountains edged the plateau on all sides except to the south, where only in the great distances could lofty peaks be seen again.

The air was warm, having none of the coolness and sweetness of the high pines. But it was not the heat of the low country and desert. Mountain quail rose from the brown grasses and gray brush, startled by their approach. Here was waterless country, and Gordon, loving the green meadows of his pines with their swift-rushing mountain brooks, told McGregor, "This tableland has never been for me. One look at it and I'm always anxious to pick up my supplies at the store and get back home."

For two more hours they traveled across the plateau, their feet and Goldie's hoofs sending up dust that clung to the warm air for some time before settling over their tracks. Finally they reached a dirt road which came from the mountain foothills to the north and continued across the plateau to Leesburg. They had walked it for an hour when the boy said, "My headache's back. Could we rest a couple of minutes?"

They sat down by the side of the road. A few miles ahead was Leesburg. "Don't go expecting much," Gordon warned. "There's a general store, a few houses, and a hotel. Leesburg sets in the middle of nowhere, and as far as I can see has no reason for being except for the likes of myself . . . and the Allen ranch," he added as an afterthought.

From the direction of the northern foothills came a

small, open truck. Gordon said, "It's Cruikshank. Maybe he'll give you a ride into town. It'll save you walking a few miles."

The truck was still more than a mile from them, but Gordon got to his feet. "Don't figure on the ride until you get it," he said. "Cruikshank is a peculiar guy. He might not even slow down for us. He's a horse trader, but with nothing ever good to trade. He's been in these parts, living up in the foothills there, for twenty or more years, I hear. He's always been after the ranch property Allen has now, but never had enough money to swing the deal. Consequently, he's been bitter toward anyone who has ever owned the ranch. Now it's Allen's turn. I heard he's uglier toward Allen than he's been with any of the other ranch owners. I suppose that's because Allen is an Easterner. Or maybe it's because Cruikshank is getting older, and still isn't any closer to buying good pasture land for his horses than he was twenty years ago. He knows everyone in town dislikes him for his bitterness, and now he's blaming Allen for it. But Allen hardly knows the guy is alive. Allen's too busy minding his own business to pay any attention to what people, even Cruikshank, think of him."

The boy suddenly got to his feet. "Cruikshank is pulling something behind the truck. Doesn't it look like a horse to you?"

"I thought it was just the dust from his wheels, but now that you mention it . . ."

The truck had reached a turn in the road. Behind and just a little to the left of the truck they were now able to

see a tied horse. He was galloping hard to keep up with
the speeding truck. He slipped coming off the turn, and
the dust behind him billowed greater than ever as his
haunches scraped the road. Somehow he managed to get
his hind legs beneath him again. The truck increased its
speed, and the horse was unable to keep up with it. He
fell again.

"He's being dragged to his death!" Gordon exclaimed.
But he found he was speaking to himself. The boy had left
his side, and was running down the road toward the
truck. He shouted to him, but McGregor kept running.

The boy found himself nearing the truck without
knowing exactly what he intended to do. He had acted
strictly on impulse. He waited until the truck was only a
few feet from him, until he heard the sudden drag of
wheels as the brakes were jammed on, and then he flung
himself to the side of the road to avoid being hit. He
landed on his hands and knees. He saw the angry face
within the cab, and heard the oaths that were shouted at
him. As the truck started up again, he sprang from a
crouched position and his hands hit the side rails.

He thought the pull of the truck had wrenched his arms
from their sockets. Yet he held on, his feet dragging while
the truck picked up speed again. His eyes located the
horse behind the vehicle. The animal had his legs under
him, but it would be only a few minutes before he'd go
down again . . . for good this time. McGregor knew it. So
must the man behind the wheel. There was no doubt now
that Cruikshank meant to *murder* this horse! The truck
swept past Gordon without slowing down.

Seeing the animal's straining, wet body and the blinded, lusterless eyes gave McGregor the strength and will to pull his feet onto the lower rail. He moved back until he was able to reach the rope. He was familiar with the knot. He knew that one good pull on the hanging end would untie it. He yanked the end hard, and the rope was whipped from the truck. He saw the horse go down, and then the dust swirled and blanketed the road behind.

He knew he couldn't jump off with the truck going so fast. There was no window in the back of the cab, so Cruikshank didn't know he had lost his victim . . . not yet. But soon. The truck went faster. Cruikshank had meant this to be the end.

Behind them and coming from the south, McGregor saw three men on horseback, riding at full gallop. They were headed for the fallen horse, and the boy was glad that others besides Gordon and himself had seen what Cruikshank had intended to do.

The outlying houses of Leesburg were less than a mile away when the truck came to a sudden stop. McGregor knew why. Cruikshank did not intend to drag a dead horse into town.

The boy jumped off the back of the truck, but did not run. He saw the door open and the man coming toward him. He saw Cruikshank's gaze shift to the back of the truck, and then quickly return to him again. He saw wild, sunken eyes, a lean and gaunt body covered with tattered clothes. He saw the haggard face and the big, worn hands, the blackened skin that must have been very wet a short while ago for now it was caked with dust. He felt sudden pity for this ragged, unkempt form in front of him . . . this worn man with the big eyes of terrible gloom.

But then the hot flame of anger burned within him again at the thought of this man's viciousness, at the agony he had caused a horse, at the murder he had intended to commit! McGregor had time to see the warning look in the man's eyes. He dodged the hands, but Cruikshank threw himself at him, catching hold of his leg. For a moment the man just held him on the ground, breathing heavily over him, and then pulled him roughly to his feet.

He never knew what Cruikshank intended to do, for suddenly the man stood still as a small sedan came down the road from town, slowing as it neared the truck and then coming to a stop before it. The boy saw a heavy-set man get out. He saw a gray suit, a gray sombrero, and then *the bright silver star of the sheriff's office on the man's lapel.*

Sudden panic seized McGregor. He ripped Cruikshank's hands from his shirt, and began to run. He tripped over some brush, and went down hard. He was getting up on his feet when he was shoved back down on the ground again. This time it was the sheriff who held him there. He heard him ask, "What are you up to now, Cruikshank? What have you got on this boy?"

"I was bringin' a horse into town to sell. This kid set him loose a piece back."

"Set him loose?"

"The colt warn't clean broke yet. I had some trouble

loadin' him so I jus' tied him up to the back, an' wuz leadin' him in.''

"And this boy untied him deliberately? Where's your horse now?''

"No tellin' where he be now. Lost for good, I reckon, unless I kin track him down, an' there ain't much chance o' that if he gits to the stones.''

"Is that right, boy? You turned his horse free?''

The boy didn't answer, and the sheriff finally turned away to look back up the road. McGregor was conscious of Cruikshank's large eyes studying him as he lay there; they looked into him, seeing the fear of the sheriff that gripped him and closed his mind to everything but a way to get free, to run again.

The sheriff turned to Cruikshank. "It don't make sense. Why would this kid want to set your horse loose?''

"I dunno anything about that. He did, an' ain't that enough?'' Cruikshank's eyes were shifty. He'd had dealings with the sheriff often. The sheriff was against him. Everybody was against him. He'd get even. Someday he'd get even with them all . . . with the whole town.

The sheriff got to his feet, and his hands left the boy.

"I can roll now," McGregor thought frantically. *"I can get away, if I move fast enough. I'll get to the mountains. They'll never catch me there. It's my only chance."*

"Better watch'm,'' Cruikshank warned. "He'll get away on ya.''

"I'm not worried,'' the sheriff said. "Besides, here comes your horse.''

Slowly, the moving figures of horses and men came up the road.

McGregor turned quickly toward them. He knew that he didn't have to run now. Gordon and Goldie were there. Gordon would help him.

"Stay where you are, Cruikshank," the sheriff said suddenly. "You wouldn't want to leave without your horse, would you?"

The boy turned to the gaunt figure that had moved toward the truck. He felt a sense of pity for Cruikshank steal over him again. Anger had left the man's large eyes, and only gloom was there once more. Cruikshank must have lost his head while trying to load his unbroken horse. His fury had mounted until his crazed mind had told him that his only recourse was to kill the animal who had defied him. Now Cruikshank was caught and cornered, and looking for escape . . . or pity.

McGregor turned to the small group that had reached them. He saw the beaten horse again. The animal was as lean and gaunt as Cruikshank and, in addition, bleeding and torn, and almost dead. McGregor's anger at this man flared again. He had no chance to speak out in his condemnation of Cruikshank's viciousness, for one of the riders dismounted just then, his face red with fury as he eyed Cruikshank and spoke to the sheriff. "Tom," he said, "I want you to arrest Cruikshank. I charge him with one of the cruelest attempts to murder a horse I've ever seen. He was dragging this colt to his death. I'll press charges all the way. I have witnesses . . . Mike, Joe, and Slim. Cruikshank would have gotten away with it, if it hadn't been for this kid here. He set the colt loose. We saw him do it."

Cruikshank's big eyes held terrible hate and bitterness

for the man who had spoken out against him. His great hands reached for his informer.

They all closed in upon Cruikshank then, pinning his long arms to his side and handcuffing his wrists behind him. The sheriff took him away as with oaths and screams he threatened vengeance on the man half his size and weight who had succeeded in sending him to jail for his crime.

Now this thin, small-boned man helped McGregor to his feet and said, "It took a lot of nerve to do what you did, kid."

McGregor looked gratefully at the man, who wore rimless eye glasses. Then Gordon was beside him, and he knew there was nothing more to fear. He looked past them to the short-coupled, dark bay horse with the white feet which the man had ridden. He watched the animal toss his head, trying to break away from the cowboy who held him.

"This is Mr. Allen," Gordon was saying. "He's the man who owns the ranch I told you about."

McGregor hardly heard Gordon. He was watching the horse, and trying to remember. A tossing head, pitched ears . . . all so familiar, yet seemingly an eternity ago. Where had he known such things as these?

Allen said, "Slim tells me you're looking for a job."

Slim? Oh, yes, Gordon was Slim. Gordon was Slim the Burro Man. McGregor put a hand to his head.

Allen spoke again. "Can you ride? Have you ever worked on a ranch before?"

"I—I d-don't . . ."

Gordon interrupted quickly, answering for him. "I'm sure he'll work out well, Allen. After all, one doesn't do what he just did for that colt without a genuine *feeling* for horses."

"Yes, that's more important than anything else. That's what counts," Allen agreed. "Well, you've got a job if you want it, kid. What's your name again?"

"McGregor. My name is McGregor." It came so easy now.

"You can start any day you like," Allen said.

The boy felt Gordon's hands on his shoulder, prodding him. But it wasn't necessary. He was looking at the fine, dark bay horse as he said, "I'll start now. I'll go along with you right away."

The horse neighed in his impatience to be turned loose. And, listening to him, McGregor knew that he had found the beginning of the road back.

Night Cry!

10

Two weeks later McGregor sat with Mike and Joe around a small open campfire. For a while he listened to their stories. They had a lot to say, but most of it was about themselves, and he'd heard it all before. As usual they were in high spirits, for their work was easy and fun for them. All they had to do was to watch the small band of mares, making sure none of them strayed or got into trouble.

It was an hour before sunset, but with the air already turning cold they had started the fire. They were a thousand feet above the plateau, and on a gently sloping range where grazing was rich and water plentiful. The band seldom moved beneath the clear sun and sky. A mile or so beyond, cattle were grazing as peacefully as were the mares. McGregor made out the forms of the

122

men riding slowly around the large herd. In the first week he had spent with them he had learned he was the worst kind of an amateur at handling cattle. He knew for certain he'd never had anything to do with steers before. For a few days Allen had watched him work, and then wisely had assigned him to Mike and Joe in caring for the broodmare band. Actually it was a job to be envied, for Allen's first love was the horses, and their care and handling took precedence over all other ranch activities.

Below on the broad plateau were more cattle and men. Beyond was the ranch house with its corrals and barns. McGregor saw the dust being raised in the largest corral, and knew Allen had put out Hot Feet for a while. The dark bay colt was Allen's most prized possession. He had bought him as a weanling, raised him, and last year had seen him win his championship. All the mares in the band would be bred to Hot Feet, and hope was running high that still other champions would come from these matings.

The boy lay back on his blanket, hands beneath his head. He caught part of Mike's story, *". . . an' that little horse threw me so high I hit a blackbird flyin' above the ring . . ."* He knew that one. So did Joe, but Joe was listening to Mike's grand tale as though hearing it for the first time. The boy glanced at the mares to make certain they were all right, and then closed his ears to the conversation.

Two weeks had gone by. Two weeks on the right road back. But where was it taking him? Would he ever see Gordon again? He *must,* for Gordon had the stolen money in his bureau drawer. He'd have to get it when he remembered to whom it belonged. He'd have to return it, wouldn't he? Maybe he wouldn't. Maybe he'd forget it. Maybe he'd just stay here. He didn't want to go to jail.

He was getting well. Slowly, yes, but getting there. His headaches came only once a day now, and sometimes not at all if he was careful not to exert himself too much.

He thought of Cruikshank. Cruikshank had gone to jail for attempting to drag that colt to his death. He'd gotten twenty-one days. He'd be more bitter than ever when he got out. But that wasn't *his* concern.

Wasn't it, though? Hadn't he helped send Cruikshank to jail? Did he now feel any sympathy for him? No, none at all. Instead he was glad Cruikshank was paying for his cruelty, his viciousness. Yet, was he any better than Cruikshank? Wasn't he looking for sympathy, kindness and understanding from others? *Wasn't he trying to avoid paying for his crime?*

He accepted all this. He knew he felt as he did about Cruikshank because the man's crime had been against a horse who could not defend himself. It made a difference. It was the reason he felt no sympathy for Cruikshank.

Horses were linked to his past, all right. He knew it now. He had known it when he had seen Hot Feet shifting so nimbly on his hoofs behind Allen and the sheriff that first day. He had been certain of it when they'd arrived at the ranch, and he had been given a horse to ride and tend. He remembered sitting in the saddle for a long time without moving, his knees pressed close against the small roan's body, his hands on the soft neck. Something had tried to get through to him then. It had tried to pierce that black, mental barrier. He had struggled, trying to help it come, and had failed again.

Allen had looked up at him. "We ride with longer stirrups here," he'd said. "But suit yourself. Ride any way you like."

Short stirrups. Leaning more forward in his saddle than the others. Something uncomfortable, uneasy about the deep Western saddle and the high pommel in front. Then and even now, two weeks later. Why? *Why?*

He rose from the blanket and moved closer to the fire. He was tired of asking himself these questions, tired of groping, tired of searching for answers that always evaded him. He would try no more. From now on he would resign himself to waiting alone, waiting for the answers to come of their own accord. No more thinking about it. No more struggling.

While he looked into the small flames of the campfire, Gordon's words came back to him: *"Some people have memory failure because they don't want to remember. If you want your memory back you've got to keep trying. You must want it back and make every effort to get it back. It's up to you. . . ."*

All right, face it. Maybe he wasn't in such a hurry any more. This was a good life, here on the ranch. He didn't want to leave, to run again. No one bothered him here. No one asked him questions about his past. Only the present was important here, and one day was very much like another.

"Hey, Mac. McGregor!"

It was Mike calling him, and he turned away from the fire. "Yes?"

"You're not being very sociable, Mac."

"I was thinking about something."

"You think too much," Mike said. "C'mon over here an' talk."

He went and sat down beside Mike. Mike Riso, the dark-haired, dark-eyed Italian who three years ago had been a barber in New York City. He watched Mike fill his pipe, packing down the tobacco before lighting. Mike with the big, floppy sombrero, the silk handkerchief about his bull neck, the riding chaps about his legs, and the boots, those high-heeled boots. Somehow, Mike looked as though he'd always worn such clothes. He wished his own Western outfit felt and looked as familiar. But it didn't. These clothes were strange to him and . . . He stopped abruptly. He had promised himself not to think about it any more. No more struggling, he'd decided.

Mike put his arm around the boy's shoulders, and pulled him roughly toward himself and his partner. "Did you know Joey and me and Allen were once known as the 'Bronx Busters'?" he asked.

"No, I didn't, Mike," McGregor replied. He looked at Joe. Joe Riley, the ex-pharmacist of a New York City drug store. Sandy-haired and light-complexioned but no taller, no larger than Mike or Allen. Allen, Irv Allen, the former owner of a New York City gasoline station. What a strange group these three were. Yet he knew more about them than he did about himself.

"You know why?" Mike asked.

McGregor looked up, startled. "Why what?" He had forgotten what they were talking about.

"What I just said!" Mike shouted impatiently. "Why we were called the 'Bronx Busters'?"

"No, I don't know . . ."

Mike jabbed his elbow into Joe's chest, and they laughed together. "We lived in the Bronx, in New York City," he said, between chuckles. "But there's a lot more to it than that. Get this, Mac! We not only lived in the Bronx, but we gave a *Wild West rodeo show* every Sunday in the Bronx!"

"Weather permitting," Joe reminded him.

"Sure. Weather permitting," Mike went on. "Anyway, we had a rodeo. Think of it, Mac! Right smack in the heart of New York City we had a rodeo every Sunday for years!"

"You're serious?" the boy asked.

"Sure I am! Allen had three vacant lots he owned, and we put up some galvanized tin sheds. That's where we kept the Bronx Bronc, Big Brother and Little Sid."

The boy could only look at Mike, stare at him, wondering if perhaps he wasn't being kidded after all. But no, Mike was deadly serious.

"Don't forget our corral," Joe prompted.

"Sure," Mike said, "the biggest corral, the *only* corral in New York City. And every Sunday, people came to stand around the corral an' watch . . ."

"Lots more watched from the windows of the apartment houses all around us," Joe said.

Mike turned to Joe. "Are you going to tell Mac this story or am I?" he asked angrily.

"All right. You tell it your way then," Joe said. "But don't leave out any of the facts, the *pertinent* facts."

Mike turned again to the boy. "Anyway, Mac. We put on this show every Sunday like I said. Allen rode the Bronx Bronc . . ."

"A big brown horse," Joe interrupted again. "Allen could really get him to buck."

"An'," Mike said, "I rode Big Brother, the most ferocious bull in . . ."

"Dehorned he was," Joe said, "as an extra safety precaution for Mike."

Mike pushed Joe away. "An' the third act was Joey here bulldoggin' Little Sid. He . . ."

"It was the only act," Joe said, "that brought the crowd to its feet every Sunday! That's because we had to have a new Little Sid each year. Little Sid had to be a calf, and calves grow. So every year we had a new one for my act. Little Sid was the only member of our cast who didn't have years of rodeo experience behind him. That's why the crowd never knew what to expect from our act."

"You either," Mike said sarcastically. "Anyway, Mac. It was a good show we put on until they made us quit."

Joe said, "A group of people in a new apartment house got together, and made up a petition against the *'noise, odors and actions of grown men playing cowboy every Sunday.'* That's the way they put it," he added in disgust. "The police *had* to do something even though they'd been enjoying the rodeos as much as everyone else. So they made us quit, an' we had to send the Bronx Bronc, Big Brother and Little Sid off to a friend of ours in Jersey."

The boy looked from Joe to Mike, and then said, because he felt he was expected to say it, "That's a sad ending."

"Not so sad at all, when you think of what it finally made us do," Mike said.

"But years later," Joe added.

"Yeah," Mike said, "but we did it, an' that's what counts."

"Did what?" McGregor asked.

"Came here," Mike returned. "Y'see, Mac, not long after our rodeo was shut down, the city finished a new bridge connecting the Bronx to Long Island. First thing we knew . . ."

"*Allen* knew, you mean," Joe said.

"Yeah, first thing Allen knew was that he was makin' money hand over fist at his gas station because it was located on the approach to the bridge."

"An' his three vacant lots were on the approach too," Joe said. "Real estate values doubled, then tripled. This wasn't due only to the new bridge traffic. Y'see, a lot of people started moving to our neighborhood just so they could get out of New York weekends by crossing the bridge and getting to the Long Island beaches."

"Whose story is this?" Mike asked furiously.

"Your story," Joe said. "But don't forget the pertinent facts, like I said before."

"Well, Mac," Mike said, "Allen held on to his station and vacant lots for a couple of years and then sold out. He came to us, and offered to set us up in a new business."

"Out west," Joe said.

"Out west," Mike repeated, "where folks appreciated the same things we did, horses and cattle. So here we are, an' here we've been for three years, thanks to the good old rodeo days."

"Thanks to the Bronx-Long Island Bridge," Joe added. "Thanks to Stark Realtors, Incorporated, specializing in fine western properties for Easterners. And, most important, thanks to Irv Allen."

"An' thanks to me," Mike said, "the ranch foreman."

"You're just a figurehead," Joe said, "an' you know it. Hank Larom is the real boss. What do you know about cattle? Nothing. Allen's smart. He picked a good man like Larom to run things, and then he gives you a fancy title to keep you happy."

"Oh, I don't know about that," Mike said, his feelings hurt. He turned to the boy and all his zeal came back. "How about that for a story, Mac? What do you think of the 'Bronx Busters' now?"

"I think it's a great story," McGregor said. He let the subject drop by getting to his feet and going to the saddle racks. Darkness was falling fast, and the well-polished leather reflected the glow of the campfire. He got a bucket and went to a nearby spring for water. It was his turn to cook tonight. Far down the range he saw the glows of other campfires, and from farther beyond came the wail of a coyote. He turned to the mares. There was plenty of good grass and water for them here. They never strayed very far. Tonight he had the watch from midnight until four o'clock, so he'd climb into his sleeping bag right after supper.

He went back to the fire, and Mike and Joe, their faces crimsoned by the flames, looked up at him.

"Joey was just sayin'," Mike said, "that the folks out here haven't accepted us even after three years. An' I told him it didn't matter 'cause we haven't accepted them yet, either. We're independent, we are."

"We can afford to be on Allen's money," Joe said. "If it wasn't for him, it'd be different, all right."

Mike withdrew his pipe, and spat in the fire. "Well, we're helpin' him make the ranch a payin' business, aren't we? He's got more money now than he had when we came."

"Thanks to Hank Larom managing things, and Allen's good sense," Joe said quietly. "It was Allen who hired Hank, and Allen who bought Hot Feet as a weanling."

Mike sucked his pipe thoughtfully. "Yep," he said. "*We're* sure beatin' these Westerners at their own game. Here *we* got a payin' cattle ranch an' the best little quarter horse in the country. That's what gets 'em, Mac, *our* havin' Hot Feet. Folks out here expect most anyone to be able to raise cattle and make a profit, but it's raisin' a grand horse like Hot Feet that makes 'em mad. Beatin' them at their own game, that's what *we're* doin', all right."

McGregor put the kettle on the two flat iron bars over the fire, and then he went to the bag of provisions.

"What you fixin' us tonight, Mac?" Mike asked.

"Boiled rice and steak."

"An' onions?"

"Sure."

Mike lay back on his blanket. "Good," he said.

The mares nickered, but they were settling down for the night. Mike and Joe as usual had talked their fill, and they would be more or less quiet until morning. McGregor got his pans ready. He found he liked to cook, even had a knack for it. And the one who cooked never had to wash the dishes. He'd be resting after supper, taking it nice and easy while Mike and Joe scrubbed the pots and plates. It was a good life and, most important to him, one set apart from the rest of the world. The wind beat against the hanging utensils, rattling them until he removed them from their hooks. It became quiet, and he felt a sense of aloofness from everything. It was as he wanted it.

Mike spoke from behind him, his voice shattering the peaceful stillness. "Y'know, Mac, between you an' me I think Allen's got somethin' else in mind for you. He's never been happy about puttin' a professional jockey up on Hot Feet like he had to do last year in the big race. I remember he said at the time, 'Mike, it's a crime to spend years raisin' a horse, givin' him the best you got in you, and then have to turn him over to some little stranger you don't know a thing about in order to race him.'"

The boy froze, a cooking utensil in one hand.

"So what I think Allen has in mind is for you to ride Hot Feet in the races comin' up at Preston," Mike continued. "He as much as told me so the other day, sayin' you were a natural born race rider, usin' such short stirrups, and sittin' like you do."

McGregor never said a word. His feeling of aloofness had been destroyed. He knew that if Mike was right, *if Allen made him ride Hot Feet at Preston, somebody might identify him as the boy wanted by the Utah state police,* and he would only have to run again. The night air became cold, chilling him.

Shortly before midnight Joe came to him, telling him it was time to get up. He hadn't slept. Without a word to Joe, he went to his hobbled horse, and saddled him quickly. Later he rode quietly out to where the band grazed and sat there, watching and thinking. An hour passed, and then another with only the wild sounds of the night to keep him company, to remind him that his job was to keep the mares from straying too far away. He rode around the band, keeping it together, listening to the sound of teeth cropping grass.

He didn't know how long he'd been on watch when he became aware of the mares' sudden restlessness. They weren't moving, but all had stopped grazing; their nostrils were blown out, sniffing the air. Some animal scent was coming to them, yet they seemed unafraid. Whatever it was created more interest than fear in them. McGregor waited a few minutes, and then, when their uneasiness continued, rode quickly back to alert Mike and Joe.

"Something's up," he said, awakening them. They rolled from their sleeping bags with no complaints. They knew their jobs.

When he got back to the band, the mares were still facing the unbroken ridge of high trees rising to the west. They were moving now, but in no particular direction.

They encircled each other, their eyes leaving the western ridge for seconds only, their nostrils still wide and quivering.

Mike and Joe rode up, taking their positions about the band. There was nothing to fear now. Working together they'd be able to keep the mares in hand and protect them. Protect them from what? Nothing that human eyes could see. Nothing a human nose could smell.

For a long time the mares continued to be restless. Flashing eyes, manes, and tails. Moving hoofs and nostrils. Then suddenly their action became faster, their eyes brighter. And with this came the scream, low at first and then mounting, becoming more and more shrill until it was the loudest and clearest of whistles. It claimed the high, unbroken ridge for its own and then rocked the air about. It lasted for a good many seconds, and then died slowly over the distant, rolling plain.

The men had no time to think about it then. The mares were moving to the west, and they rode after them, turning them back, holding them together until they had them quiet once more. Now the night was deathly still. The mares kept their heads up, sniffing the air for a long while before losing interest and grazing again. The scent, like the scream, was gone.

McGregor sat on his horse, looking over at the western ridge. Everything was as it had been before except that Mike and Joe were now beside him.

"What kind of a scream was that?" Mike asked. "Sure no animal I ever heard before."

"Could have been a bird," Joe suggested. "Maybe an eagle."

Mike shrugged his shoulders. "Maybe so, Joey. Anyway, it's gone."

"But we'd better stick together the rest of the night," Joe said. "It might come back, and it sure made the mares act queer. Yeah, Mike, we'd better stay with Mac. We don't want anything happening to the mares. We sure don't, not with Allen coming around early tomorrow morning."

They turned to the boy, watching him as he continued to gaze at the western ridge. "Whatcha lookin' at, Mac?" Mike asked. "Whatcha thinkin'?"

"That was a horse we heard," the boy said quietly. "A stallion . . . a wild stallion."

"You're kiddin'." Mike turned to Joe, laughing. "The kid's kiddin', Joe!"

"Maybe he isn't," Joe said. "Mac, are you sure? Have you ever heard a horse scream like that before?"

A minute passed, then another. They didn't think McGregor was going to answer. Finally his words came, so low they could hardly hear them. "Yes, I've heard a horse scream like that . . . a long, long time ago."

One more step on the road back. *He had recognized the whistle of a wild stallion. Where had he heard it before?*

Joe said, "I don't think you're right, but it's sure going to give Allen something to worry about when we tell him in the morning."

"It was an owl, that's what it was," Mike said. "I guess I know an owl when I hear one."

The boy glanced at him but said nothing.

The Black Outlaw

11

Dawn came with the paling of the eastern sky, and with the red flash of the sun Allen arrived on the upland range. He rode his champion, and the small, dark bay was still full of run after his long climb. Hot Feet came toward the camp with a graceful sweep, his strides short but quick. He tossed his head as though furious with Allen for sitting so upright in the saddle and creating more wind resistance.

Allen was urging him on, but his seat in the saddle lent no help to the running horse. His shouts pealed up and down the range. He kept Hot Feet in full stride until he was only a few yards from the dying campfire, and then he raised the reins. The small horse came to an abrupt, plunging halt.

As he witnessed this amazing, sudden stop from a full gallop, the boy remembered Gordon's saying, "Sure, the quarter horse is fast over short distances. And he's quick and easy to handle. He's a *type* developed to work the range, but he's no race horse. The thoroughbred is the race horse.''

Maybe Gordon would have told all this to Allen, and maybe not. The boy knew only that such words would never come from him. He realized this simply by looking into Allen's eyes, and seeing the love and pride that shone there for Hot Feet. The small horse had his ears back and his feet were pounding the ground, sending up dust clouds. Just beyond were the mares, their heads held aloft, their ears cocked forward, watching him.

'' 'Morning, boys,'' Allen said, but his eyes were only for the mares, and the love he had for Hot Feet was bestowed upon them as well. He, more than Mike and Joe, had become a part of the West. He had been wise in listening to men far more experienced than he, and through them he had selected the right ranch, cattle and hands to make this new venture pay for itself. In those early days, only the purchase of the weanling Hot Feet had been his decision alone. He had seen the potential speed in the small colt when others had shaken their heads. So Allen, more than anyone else, shared Hot Feet's glory when the championship had been won last year. Afterward he had traveled throughout Arizona, and to California, New Mexico and Texas, selecting brood-mares he *alone* felt best suited for Hot Feet's court. His ranch and cattle were making him rich, but his sole joy was Hot Feet and the mares. Through them he had found his place, his niche in the West.

Only when Mike began telling him of the band's

restlessness during the night did he turn away from the mares. At first he was curious and only mildly interested, but he became genuinely concerned when Mike attempted to explain what the eerie scream had sounded like.

Mike ended with, "It could have been an owl. I guess it coulda been that, Irv."

"Too shrill for an owl," Joe said. "My guess is that it was an eagle. But Mac here says . . ." He stopped, and turned to the boy. "Maybe you'd better tell him, Mac."

The boy turned from Joe to Allen. He saw that Mike's and Joe's suggestions had failed to wipe out the concern that still showed in the man's eyes. Mares didn't react the way these had from nocturnal sounds made by an owl or an eagle. Allen knew this, and so did he.

"Yes, Mac," Allen said. "What do *you* think it was?"

"A stallion." He saw the fear come quickly, brightly to the man's eyes. He saw the sudden stiffening of Allen's seat in the saddle, and the tightening of his legs about Hot Feet, sending him dancing again.

Mike's and Joe's eyes shifted nervously from the boy to Allen, and then back again. The swinging of their legs in their long stirrups indicated the stress they too felt because of Allen's reaction to McGregor's reply.

Allen finally spoke. "You're sure?" he asked. He felt both cold and hot. His gaze never left the boy, and he realized that McGregor didn't need to answer him. The boy was certain of what he'd heard. He couldn't question those eyes.

Mike said, "Joey and I think the kid's all mixed up,

Irv. There ain't no wild horses in this section. We know that, all right, same as you do.''

Allen's eyes were on the western ridge. He removed his glasses to wipe them, then put them on again. "No, Mike," he said, "we don't know that at all. Lots of things could be up in that country without our knowing."

"But Hank Larom would know," Mike insisted, "an' all the other guys who've lived around here longer'n we have. They've said lots of times, and you've heard them, that any wild mustangs around here were long ago driven up into the roughest part of the country, an' have either been starved or hunted to death by wolves 'n mountain lions."

Allen never took his eyes off the high ridge as he said, "I'm not thinking of mustangs, Mike."

"Then you ain't got anything else to worry about!" Mike attempted a short laugh. "We're here, boss. We won't let anything happen to 'em. Will we, Joey?"

Allen said, "I had a letter yesterday from a friend of mine over in Pueblo . . . that's about fifty miles east of here. He said a wild, outlaw horse had stolen two of his best mares."

Mike laughed again. "They prob'ly just roamed away from his men, Irv. I guess he don't have good men like you do. I guess not."

"No, Mike. He saw them go."

"Y'mean he saw the stallion, Irv?" Joe asked.

"Yes. It was night but he caught a glimpse of him. He said he wasn't any mustang but big and black, coal black. The horse ran faster than he'd ever seen one run before, and took the mares with him. They chased them, but he was too smart. They lost the tracks.''

"You're kiddin', Irv. Aren't you kiddin'?" Mike asked.

"Why would I want to kid you?" Allen's voice was impatient, angry. He turned again to the western ridge. "That wild outlaw might have come over here. He might even be out there now."

"You're crazy," Mike said. Now he wasn't speaking to his employer but to Irving Allen, who had owned the gasoline station not far from his own barbershop four years ago in New York City. "Y'been readin' too many westerns. You're wild and woolly like they are . . . an' those days are done with, Irv."

After a few minutes Allen turned to him, and then his gaze shifted to Joe, and finally came to rest on the boy. He said, "Mac, I want you to spend the day up on the ridge. If you find any sign of *him* I want to know . . . any sign at all . . . tracks, anything. If he's out there I must do something about him." One hand stroked Hot Feet's glistening neck, and when he had finished speaking he turned to look at the mares again. All his concern and fear were for them, for they were meant for his champion alone.

An hour later McGregor was riding up the ridge. The slope at first was open and very gradual. His horse became impatient with the slow walk at which he was holding him. He was being careful, for the terrain was covered with small angular rocks and high clods of bunch-grass on which his mount could easily trip. Finally he gave him his head, and was amazed at the way the little quarter horse chose his ground, picking his feet well up and over the rocks and brush-grass, his short strides sure and never faltering.

When the ascent became steep McGregor brought him down to a walk again. Soon they moved through dim forest aisles no different from the mountain range to the east of the plateau, which McGregor had known with Gordon. Above him came the sound of the whistling wind through the treetops. Beyond, and ever upward, was the high country with its majestic peaks.

"Go only to the top of the timber line," Allen had instructed him, "and in the direction you think the scream came from. If you see *his* tracks or any indication at all that he's been there, come back and tell us. Tomorrow we'll make up a party and go after him, providing you find anything. You'll be able to sight everything from up there. He'll have mares with him, so if he's around you ought to find some indication of their movements. If not, just come back. Maybe Joe was right after all. Maybe what you heard *was* an eagle."

No, it was a stallion he'd heard. He was certain of that. He'd swear to it. But why was he so sure?

For many long hours he climbed, and only the horse's body working between his legs was familiar to him. He had a gun in his holster, and he supposed he'd be able to use it if he had to. But it was a strange, hanging weight at his side. On the saddle's pommel was his lariat, and he thought he would be even more awkward using that if he needed it. His sole confidence rested in the intelligence of the horse carrying him and in his own riding ability.

The trees thinned as he neared the top of the ridge, and soon he was in high, open country. The stallion could have been somewhere up here last night. He looked down, his eyes roving over the pine trees below and over the grazing range still farther below. He saw the far-off figures of the mares and cattle. His gaze turned to the land about him, land stripped bare of everything but dry brush and rock. It was going to be hard to find any tracks here, but he needed to see only a scratch on the weathered stone, the merest indication that a horse's hoofs had trod here. That was all Allen wanted to know.

Even at this high altitude the air was warmed by the late afternoon sun. It was still, very still, and the great stone ramparts above him, reflecting all the gold of the sun's rays, were blazing and glorious. He suddenly forgot to look for the tracks of a stallion. He welcomed this silent loneliness. There was no sound, only the great solitude of the upper air. He forgot Gordon and Allen, Joe and Mike. He forgot completely his recent life, the only life he remembered. For the time being he felt absolutely free and alone and secure. Nothing could be so wonderful as this, nothing so thrilling as that world which lay above him. He turned his horse away from the world below.

He climbed toward the great, glowing pinnacles without knowing why he went. His horse moved very carefully over the rugged ground, making no attempt to move faster than a slow walk. McGregor let him pick his way. He knew he must be over ten thousand feet high. He felt he could almost touch the floating cakes of snowy clouds. And above the clouds rose the highest of the peaks.

Finally he entered a narrow stone aisle palisaded by tremendous cliffs of granite.

It was there he brought his horse to a stop. It was there he came to his senses, and asked himself *why* had he come? To sit his horse on top of the world? Was this his only answer?

He remembered the tracks he had been sent to look for. He remembered Allen's orders not to go any higher than the timber line already two thousand feet below him. He had been told that beyond the crest of this range was the land of the great canyons, seldom touched and unknown. Perhaps that's why he had come to look upon these lands, for he too was unknown.

Since he had come this far, he decided to go to the crest. He urged his horse on again, continuing to climb, and the cliffs closed in upon him. Finally he came to the end of the ascent and the canyon country was there for him to see.

For a long while he gazed upon its awesome desolateness. He made out the thin ribbon of a river meandering through the deepest of all the canyons. It turned and twisted but had no movement from this height. And then his eyes, becoming more accustomed to the fading light and shadows, saw more than desolateness, and he became conscious of more than the great void and depth and space. He saw beauty in the bold domes and the gouged, gutted, uplifted rock of varied, startling colors . . . all reds and yellows and blues. He wiped his blurred eyes to see better and looked upon it all for a long, long time.

Finally he turned away. He had seen these lands, and

now he would go back to look for hoofprints. But his gaze returned to the trail that led down the other side of the precipice. For a thousand feet it dropped sharply before becoming lost in the highest of the canyons. It was wide enough and safe. It had been used by animals and Indians long before the white man came to this country.

He was turning his horse away from it when in the loose shale, weathered to a fine sand, he saw the tracks! He left his saddle quickly and knelt on the ground. The hoofprints were large and oval-shaped. Moreover, they were clean cut, and had been made recently. There were two sets but each was made by the same hoofs. A horse had come up this trail, and then gone back to the canyons below. He had traveled alone. If he was the stallion Allen feared, where was his band?

McGregor got to his feet, and looked down the trail. If it was the same stallion he wouldn't have left his mares very far away . . . and never for very long. Had they moved on again, or were they in the first canyon just a thousand feet below from where he stood?

His job was to go back, and tell Allen what he had learned. He looked again at the hoofprints. So large, so perfect. He stared at them for a long while. He was drawn to them as he had been to the nocturnal scream that had brought him here. They beckoned him from dark, lost time. He had no choice but to follow them. Leading his horse, he started down the trail toward that first canyon.

If the steepness of the descent frightened his horse, the animal gave no indication of it. He followed him with no hesitation, balancing and placing his feet with great care on the loose shale. Only once did he slip, and he drew himself quickly back on his haunches, his feet bunched together, sliding until there was a leveling off of the trail.

The worst part of the descent was behind them. The boy looked back, knowing that in a little while he'd have to retrace his steps. They'd made short work of the first five hundred feet. Going back would take longer, but would not be so difficult. The yellow walls of the first canyon were no more than another five hundred feet away.

Why had he come this far? What did he expect to find? A stallion and his band of mares. He had decided that while above. He felt certain they'd be in the canyon ahead. Then what more did he need to know? Why hadn't he returned to the ranch? *Just to look upon them and go back?* He knew this wasn't the answer. There was something else . . . something he did not understand or even try to understand . . . something that was making him go on, just as it had done all day. He knew only that he didn't want to fight this impulse, and that he couldn't turn back.

He kept going until the canyon walls hung over him. There were no hoofprints on the bare, worn rock. But ahead, about one hundred yards or so, brush-grass and sage grew. When he arrived there, he found the hoofprints again in the dry, red earth. There were many other prints beside those great perfect hoofs of the stallion. He needed no more proof than this that the stallion and his band were here.

He mounted and rode on, stopping only at a bubbling

spring that gushed from beneath the walls. In the soft earth around the pool, the hoofprints were deep. There were also the tracks of mountain lions. A strange place. He felt for his gun to make sure he still had it, and then mounted and rode into the darkening canyon. If he had looked up at the golden spires of the top walls, he would have known it was almost sunset. But his eyes were on the ground, following the hoofprints.

He first became aware that he was nearing the band by the restlessness of his mount. The horse trembled and his head came up high with dilating nostrils. The breeze in the canyon was coming toward them, bringing scents with it. McGregor raised the hand holding the reins, and his horse came to a stop.

Not far ahead there was a twist in the canyon. He could not see what lay beyond. But he knew the stallion and his mares were there, and that they could not yet be aware of his presence. He looked around, then turned his horse back, riding to a scrub cedar growing out of the rocks. He dismounted and tied his horse securely. He didn't want him to get away.

Now he proceeded up the canyon on foot, careful to make no noise. He kept close to the high wall on his right, and finally came to the twist in the canyon. He inched forward, staying in the shadows. Just a few feet beyond was a high cleft in the wall. The trail led through this deep pass, and the ground carried the tracks of many mountain animals as well as those of horses. Through the pass he saw distant mesas and cliffs, and the endless canyons he had looked upon from above. This pass led to the far country. But the stallion and his band had not yet used it to leave the canyon.

He saw the mares at the far end of the canyon, grazing on the brown grass. All about the band hung the great cliffs which afforded no escape from this walled fortress. *If Allen and his men had come along, the stallion and his band would no longer run free.*

But the stallion. Where was he?

McGregor went forward, and beyond the pass, going slowly and staying in the deep shadows. The mares couldn't hear him or smell him because of the downwind. Finally he was able to distinguish their colors . . . bays, browns, grays, buckskins and palominos. Fifty or more of them, all sizes and kinds. Short-coupled quarter mares, lean and wiry mustangs, cow horses carrying their ranch brands, and long-limbed horses which had been used only for pleasure riding. They were all there. Some were in better physical condition than others because they had taken more readily to the wild life they had chosen, a life that had held many days without good grass and water and always constant movement.

He wondered that they stayed in this canyon, foraging on the brush-grass when they could have gone on to better grazing lands. Then he remembered Allen's quarter mares, and knew why their leader kept them here.

"But where is the stallion?" McGregor asked himself again.

He looked for him. His gaze turned to the pool, near the end of the canyon. Several mares were there but not their leader. If the stallion was feared by so many because of his great intelligence, why was he not aware of an intruder in the canyon? Why was he not watchful? And why did he have his band grazing in a place from which they could so easily be prevented from escaping? The stallion's natural instinct should have told him of the danger that threatened him and his band. Long ago his whistle of warning should have resounded through the canyon, starting his band on the move again.

A deep sense of disappointment came over McGregor. Why? Why had he expected so much more from this horse? And wasn't what he found all to the good? Couldn't he now return to the ranch and tell Allen of the simple job it would be to remove the marauding outlaw and his band from the range forever?

Yes, unless the stallion wasn't in the canyon.

McGregor's gaze left the band for the opposite wall. He looked into the deep shadows, and suddenly his body froze. He saw *him*! The stallion was only a short distance away, and he too stood as motionless as a statue. They looked at each other.

Coal black. A giant horse as they'd said. But not burly. Tall and long limbed. His great body was scarred with long running wounds that had healed only to become reopened and closed again, crisscrossed and pitiful to see. His long tail trailed to the ground and, like his mane, was thickly matted with burrs. His mouth was red-raw from thistles. His head, very small, was held high, the great eyes alert and never shifting, never leaving him for a second!

How long had the stallion been there? And why? Why

had he never uttered his shrill signal of warning to his band? Now, even now, the black horse didn't move but stood still, without thinking of escape for himself and his band!

The boy's hands clutched the flesh of his thighs. He found himself shaking, trembling. His eyes never left the stallion. Something stirred within him, and there came an inner voice from the deep, black recess of his mind. It commanded him over and over again, *"Don't move . . . wait . . . wait."* Even had he been able to move, he could not have denied this command.

Suddenly the black stallion stepped from the shadows into the last bit of light in the canyon. He came quickly to the boy, and stopped before him.

McGregor reached out to the stallion, and touched the raw mouth. As he did, words came to his lips that he did not understand, soft utterances that were meaningless to him. But the great stallion seemed to understand them, for he lowered his head still more.

McGregor sought release from the black barrier that kept him from knowing what had happened. His body trembled again. What were these utterances that came from the turmoil erupting within him? He had no control over what he said or did. Yet he knew he was talking to this stallion, and was being understood! He knew his hand was removing burrs from the long forelock, and that he had done all this before! He heard that inner voice again, that never-ending command, "Wait . . . wait . . . wait."

For how long? How long must he wait? How long before *he would know himself*?

Lone Rider

12

Once this horse had been his. That much he knew. No wild outlaw would have come and stood before him, nuzzling his hand, nickering, listening. The boy accepted this without question, and asked himself only, *"When was he mine? Where? How long ago?"*

The great stallion was familiar to him. His eyes had looked upon the wedge-shaped head with the small ears before. They knew the long, thin nostrils and the wondrous gaze that was fixed on him. They knew the slender neck with its high, mounting crest . . . the muscled withers, the great strength of back, the chest and shoulders and legs. All these his eyes had looked upon before. Just as his hands had known such touches, soft and gentle. Only his brain was the stranger.

The shadows from the lofty walls had met an hour

before, and night had come to the canyon. Yet McGregor continued standing beside the stallion, his hands on the shaggy unkempt coat as if afraid to let go lest he lose him again. He thought how much he would like to brush him and make his coat glisten. Once before it had shone beneath his hands. He knew this, too.

The air became cold. A wind stirred, and then mounted in intensity until it was whipping the stallion's heavy mane and forelock. Short neighs came from the far end of the canyon, and the stallion turned to look at the mares. But he did not leave the boy.

A low whistle and stomping of hoofs broke the stillness of the upper canyons, and McGregor remembered the horse he had tied to the scrub tree.

The black stallion turned, too, his head held high, his eyes afire. Every line of his gigantic body trembled. He was ready to go up the canyon, when the boy spoke to him in the language they alone understood. Sounds and words flowed effortlessly and without question from McGregor's lips.

The stallion screamed his shrill clarion call of challenge but did not move. He stood still for several minutes, his body trembling in his eagerness to fight. As the boy continued to talk to him, and no answering challenge care from beyond, the stallion quieted. Finally he turned again to the mares, and a few moments later he left to join them.

McGregor stood alone in the darkness, pondering the things he had to do. There was feed in the saddlebags for his horse, and biscuits left over from noontime for himself. It would do him until tomorrow.

Tomorrow? What about tomorrow? He must return to the ranch. He must tell Allen that he had found *no sign of the stallion and his band.* Somehow he would return to the canyon, for here was his past. From the black stallion he would learn all he wanted to know. *But he needed time.*

He went up the canyon to unsaddle his horse and to feed and water him. Later he returned to where he had left the stallion and started a fire. Sitting beside it, he ate the hard biscuits and waited impatiently for the hours to pass. Perhaps as early as tomorrow the door to his memory would begin to swing open for him, allowing light to penetrate the mystery of his past.

During the night he slept only for minutes and at long intervals. The stallion visited him often, his gigantic form silhouetted against the walls by the light of the small campfire. The boy never tired of feasting his eyes upon him. And when he could not see him, he heard the soft rhythmical beat of his hoofs. Through it all, he felt the great love he had for this horse. He could not sleep, knowing that the very nearness of the stallion stimulated an emotion that was strongly linked to his past. *Soon,* he thought, *it'll bring back everything I want to know.*

Dawn came to the canyon with a wan grayness, and the movements of the band were vague and shadowy. McGregor waited for the black stallion to come. When he saw him, he felt uplifted with sheer joy and love. Through the pale path of light the stallion loped so beautifully that he seemed almost unreal in the weird grayness.

McGregor had intended to look upon him just once more, and then leave the canyon. But he found he could not go. This feeling he had for the stallion was too stimulating. Would it not soon stimulate his very brain? And would he not, because of it, know everything about himself, his whole past, within *minutes?*

Sobs came from his lips when the stallion stopped before him. He threw his arms about the horse's neck and waited for the elusive mental awakening to come. But nothing came. Screams suddenly took the place of his sobs. He was desperate. He refused to listen, even to hear the inner voice that kept repeating, *"Wait . . . wait."* He knew no patience, only terrible frustration and fury at being repelled again.

He never could have told how he got on the stallion's back. He knew only that he was riding as he had ridden this great horse so often before. He burrowed into the heavy mane as if to hide from a world that would not accept him. He lay low on the stallion's back, urging him to run ever faster. Here he belonged, this much no one could take from him! He let the stallion split the band of mares in two frightened groups, let him scream and whirl, bending with him while he turned and leveled out again. His own shouts echoed the stallion's whistle. The band dropped behind them.

He rode lower and faster, up and down the canyon. The stallion kept running because he loved to run, scattering and chasing the mares in his great excitement. Finally, McGregor took him through the pass that led to the distant mesas and endless canyons.

He rode for hours, and the sun was high when he brought the stallion back through the pass and into the canyon. He was tense, glowing and excited. His blood was as heated as the stallion's. He knew so much and so little. This horse was a part of him, and he a part of this horse. They were one, yet he did not know why this was so. He did not know the stallion's name or his own. Where had they come from? Where had he ridden him as he had today . . . so many times, so long ago? Who was he? Who was the stallion?

His head was splitting. All the excitement, the hard riding had brought back the pain again. He slipped off the stallion, and put his hands to his head.

A deep depression swept over him. He knew he was not yet well, that all he could do was to wait and wait. In time the headaches would cease. In time he would remember everything.

He rubbed the stallion's nose and told him to go back to his mares, that he would return soon, and that the horse should wait for him. He stayed there, watching the stallion, until the gigantic horse had reached the mares. Then he turned and walked up the canyon. He knew it would be late in the day before he reached the ranch, and already he was a night overdue. His steps came faster and with them a growing, gnawing fear that his long hours of riding might have put the stallion and himself in danger of being found in the canyon. What if Allen and his men had set out early this morning or even last night to look for him? Might they not find his tracks and those of the stallion on the crest of the upper range?

He burst into a run when he neared his saddled horse. They must not find him or his stallion! They must leave them alone. He needed time, more time!

With frantic fingers he untied the horse. He had his foot lifted to the stirrup when he saw the riders coming down the canyon. A long line of men, they were led by Allen astride his dark bay, Hot Feet.

The Hunters

13

He mounted and rode toward them, his jaw working. He told himself that he could stop them. They were looking only for him, and now that they had found him they would return to the ranch. But as he neared the line of men he realized how wrong he was.

He saw more than Allen's grim face, concerned as it had been the day before for the safety of his mares. He saw more than the puzzled and trail-wearied eyes of Mike and Joe. For with them rode the *hunters*, men hardened by long years spent in the saddle, and their sun-blackened faces were still, disclosing nothing. But their eyes gave them away. To a man their eyes blazed with the excitement of the chase. He knew these men had found the stallion's hoofprints.

McGregor's gaze remained on Hank Larom, the ranch

foreman. Here was a man, a good man, whose deep-set eyes shone blacker and brighter than any of the others. Looking into their great depths, McGregor believed everything he'd been told about him. It was said he had run so many wild mustangs through the uplands that he thought like one. Larom, more than any of the others, was a man to be feared. Larom knew the horse trails, the water holes, the gaps and canyons. He knew how to drive a band of wild horses, and to turn them into any one of a number of traps he had set. He had been a wild-horse hunter not for profit and sale, but for the thrill of the chase.

Allen said, "Where is *he*, McGregor?"

The boy tore his eyes from Hank Larom. He looked at Allen, and answered, "He's gone. He and the mares have left the country."

Perhaps, if only Mike and Joe had been with Allen, McGregor would have been believed. But Hank Larom was there.

"We started out last night, when you didn't get back," Allen said. "We knew you'd found something."

Larom's eyes had left McGregor. He was looking down the canyon. *He knew.* The horse he rode was one the boy had never seen before. A buckskin, tough, lean, and wiry. This was no quarter horse bred by man, handled by man since the day he'd been foaled. No, this horse had been a wild mustang.

Larom's gaze swept back, found McGregor looking at his horse, and said, "Spooky is a broke wild horse, Mac. He ain't agreein' with you at all that the stud's gone.

Nope, it ain't so, he's tellin' me.''

The buckskin was snorting, He had his ears far forward and his eyes were turned down the canyon.

Larom's long jaw swung out as he added, ''No better way of knowin' what's around you than by ridin' a broke wild horse. Somehow they know plenty without seein' anything or catchin' a scent. It ain't natural, but that's the way it is. Ain't it so, Spooky?'' He patted the neck of his buckskin. *"Now let's see what's up ahead."*

The men pulled quickly out of line. The boy tried to stop them, but Allen had hold of his horse. ''Why'd you do it, Mac? What reason did you have for lying to me?'' Allen kept him with Mike and Joe while the hunters moved away.

McGregor said nothing. He could *do* nothing except follow them with his eyes. He had told his stallion to wait for him in the canyon, and had made it easy for them. Never had a better horse-trap been prepared by Larom than the one he, McGregor, had set unwittingly for his stallion.

He slid down from the saddle, and began walking after them. A minute later Allen rode beside him. ''Kid, what's come over you?'' he asked. But the boy kept quiet, his eyes never leaving the mounted riders beyond. He saw them stop a short distance from the twist in the canyon, draw together and listen to Larom's orders. Soon they were moving again. He saw the last man in line disappear around the bend. Suddenly the canyon walls vibrated with the stallion's whistle!

He ran, Allen's horse moving beside him, and then he stopped. Just ahead the hunters sat their horses across the canyon floor, closing this path of escape to the stallion. Far on the right were Hank Larom and two more men, sitting astride their mounts before the entrance to the pass, closing that means of escape, too.

It was easy, so easy. The trap had been sprung. The stallion and his band were only a short distance down the canyon. The mares were bunched, their heads together. The black stallion stood alone, just in front of his band. His head was held high, and turning constantly; he nickered to his mares. He must have realized they had no chance to scatter and break through the line of men.

The boy went to Larom. He heard the ranch foreman call to the man next to him, "Russ, look'ut that stud horse. You never before seen anything like him!" Larom's face was intensely eager. "He's somethin' I've seen in dreams, but never real, not in the forty years I've been huntin'. He's a perfect horse, a *great* horse . . . an' he's smart, Russ. He knows we got him trapped, but he's smart and waitin' to break through. He's waitin' there for us to come and get him."

Russ didn't say anything for a minute, and then, "We won't be able to get near him, Hank, not on what we're ridin'. Even your buckskin is scared to death of him. He'll never go near that hoss. He's too smart for that!"

What he said was true of all the horses in the barrier line. They were squealing in their terror of the black stallion.

Russ went on, "We got to cut him off from his band, Hank. The mares will be easy for us to handle, if we kin separate 'em."

"It's not the mares we want," Larom said. "It's *him*.

An' I ain't never goin' to quit until I git him. After him there ain't no other horse for me in the world.''

"It's goin' to be like fightin' a cougar with bare hands," Russ said. "Like I said before, we ain't gettin' our horses up to him. He'd kill 'em sure, an' they know it."

"I'll go up walkin'," Larom said.

The other rider didn't take his eyes off the stallion. "Then he'll kill you, too, Hank. You know that as well as I do. I know he's got a killer look in his eyes without even bein' able to see it from here. I know it jus' by the way he's standin' up there, an' waitin'."

"I ain't goin' to let him get away," Larom said. "I ain't, an' that's for sure." For the first time he moved the rifle he carried.

The boy saw this movement and so did Allen, who said, "Hank, we take this stallion alive or not at all. I couldn't get rid of him that way."

Larom's eyes didn't leave the stallion. "Boss, I wasn't goin' to kill that stud. I guess I'd shoot myself before I done anything like that. I was jus' thinkin' I'd *crease* him, if I couldn't git him any other way."

The other rider turned to Allen. "By *creasin'* Hank means grazin' a bullet along his neck. It would cut him down without hurtin' him much. Hank's one of the few men who can do it, boss. I've seen him."

McGregor's face twitched convulsively. He inched toward Larom's rifle. No one was going to graze his horse with a bullet. How long ago had it been since Larom had hunted horses? *Years!* And his aim needed to be off only a fraction of an inch to *kill*.

Suddenly Larom said, "The stud's comin' down!"

Every man in the line was set, with one hand controlling his frightened mount and the other on his rifle, ready to fire into the air to terrorize the stallion into going back if he sought to break out of the canyon.

The stallion came closer, the beat of his hoofs swifter and louder. The men looked and looked, following his every movement, each man longed to have him for his own. Yet in these brief moments all the hardened hunters except one gave him up as unattainable. Only Larom cherished this stallion so much that he would risk his life to capture him.

The horse came to a plunging stop a short distance away from them. He stood there watching them, his large eyes moving up and down the line of men until they found the boy. He nickered and pounded his hoofs into the earth. Every muscle of his body was clearly defined in the bright sun. His small head rocked and he tossed his mane and forelock vigorously. He nickered again, his eyes never leaving the boy.

Russ said, "He's got the killer look. I told you he'd have it, Hank. Even the hair on his neck gives him away for what he is. He'll kill you if you go after him alone, an' if we go as a group he'll break the line and scatter with his mares. We ain't seein' him again once he does that. He's too fast for our hosses. I knew that jus' seein' him come down."

"I know," Larom said, and all his great longing was in his voice. "We'll never git near him . . . not unless I kin crease him. But God, Russ, if I kill him, I won't be able to live with myself."

"Get him now, Hank. You couldn't miss at fifty ·yards."

"No, I couldn't miss at this distance." Larom slid down from his restless buckskin, and handed the reins to Russ. But he never raised his rifle, for McGregor's hands were on it, holding it down. Then he heard McGregor's words:

"I'll get him. I'll get him for you."

Then McGregor left, before Larom had a chance to understand what the boy meant to do. The foreman watched with the others, staring and unbelieving, while McGregor walked toward the stallion. He realized immediately that the kid wasn't going to his death, for the savageness had left the stallion's eyes. McGregor pulled the Black's head down to him and stayed with the stallion, stroking him, while the men stared, still not believing what they had witnessed. Finally McGregor turned away from the stallion, and came back to them.

"Give me a halter, and we'll go with you," he said.

Larom tore his incredulous gaze away from McGregor to get the halter out of his saddlebag. He gave it to the boy without saying a word.

Far down the canyon, the mares raised their heads to nicker to their leader. The stallion turned toward them but didn't move. Without him they would be free no longer, returning quickly and easily to the domestic life most of them had left at his bidding. They would follow the mounted ponies back to the ranch, eager once more for good feed and shelter and care.

The stallion turned to the boy approaching him. He, too, was ready to go home.

The men watched McGregor slip on the halter. They broke their line across the canyon when the stallion was led toward them, Allen going on ahead. Hank Larom nodded to several men, and they left to get the mares.

Russ, riding beside Larom, said quietly, "We ain't never seen anything like that before, Hank."

"No. We saw a lot of things today we ain't ever seen before."

"But that's a wild stallion. How's the kid gittin' away with it?"

Larom shrugged his thin shoulders. "I ain't knowin' how, but he gentled him some way before we got here."

"All in one night?"

"Has to be. He couldn't have come across him before late yesterday afternoon."

"It ain't right," Russ said. "It's spooky, that's what it is. Spooky."

"I know, but sometimes it happens. Sometimes it does." Larom paused. "I'd give ten years of my life if it'd happened to me, Russ . . . ten years."

"You better wait 'til you see how the kid makes out with him before sayin' that, Hank. I still wouldn't want to be in his shoes. Nope, not me."

Closing Hands

14

It was a little over a week since they had brought the black outlaw to the ranch and had given him the largest of the corrals. As long as McGregor tended him he gave no trouble, but none of the other men dared go near him. To them he remained "a wild stallion never clear broke." They knew the boy could handle him, but with the exception of Hank Larom none of them understood why this was so. They listened to Larom explain that "Sometimes it happens. Sometimes it ain't necessary to break a wild horse by ridin' him until he finds out you're the boss." They shook their heads, not believing this any more than everything else they had witnessed. They decided that sooner or later a reckoning must come. To their minds, gentle hands, and a soft voice—instead of ropes and bronc saddle—had no place in the mastery of a mature, unbroken stallion.

Although Allen hadn't forgiven McGregor for telling him that the stallion and his band had left these parts when they hadn't, he had no alternative but to put the boy in complete charge of the black horse. No one else would touch the stallion without his being fully broken. Only Larom could have broken him the way they understood, and he wouldn't do it because he was convinced it wasn't necessary. He believed that the boy and the stallion should be left alone for the time being to see how things worked out.

This arrangement suited McGregor perfectly. He had not lost his horse. He still had time to learn all he wanted to know. Early one morning when he had finished brushing the stallion, he looked around to find Allen standing outside the corral fence. Allen called to him. As he walked toward the fence he was filled with uneasiness, for he knew his employer would have fired him days ago if it had not been for Hank Larom. Was his dismissal coming now?

At the fence he said, "Yes, boss?"

Allen removed his hat with thin, nervous hands. He said nothing; his eyes were on the stallion who stood in the center of the corral, watching them.

The boy, too, turned to his horse and then back to Allen again.

Finally the man said, "You got him pretty well cleaned up in the short time he's been here."

"I can change his coat, but not the scars."

"No, they're there to stay, all right."

In the adjacent corral was the stallion's band. The mares began moving about. Their hot smell was heavy in the still air. Just beyond in another corral ran Hot Feet with tossing head. Allen's eyes turned to his prized quarter stallion, and he looked upon him as he would no other horse in the world. "The outlaw's a fine horse, but Hot Feet's a better one," he said.

"Better for you," McGregor replied quietly. "It all depends who's looking at them, and what he wants in a horse."

Allen was silent for a few moments, and then he said, "Yes, I guess that's true." He turned to raise a long, bony finger in the boy's face. "But the real men in this horse game are the breeders, the men who take the time to figure out bloodlines and crosses, who mate their mares intelligently, trying to improve their breed or type of horse."

The boy couldn't help smiling in spite of the finger wagging in his face. "Sometimes you don't get exactly what you want. Sometimes you're disappointed."

"I know that," Allen returned brusquely. "But at least we *try,* and that's what is important in this game. We spend time and thought trying to improve our stock." His eyes found the black stallion again. "I don't want *him,*" he said. "I had nothing to do with his being here. Neither did any other person. He's a product of the wild, just an accident of birth, like any one of the thousands of mustangs who've roamed this country for centuries."

"I'll take him, if you don't want him," the boy said quickly. His chest was so tight that his words came only in a whisper. Allen turned to him, and McGregor repeated what he'd said, louder this time.

The keen eyes behind the rimless glasses saw everything. Finally Allen said, "No, I'm holding on to him, Mac. For the time being, anyway."

"But you'll keep me in mind in case . . ."

"Yes, of course. You're the only one who can handle him . . . except, perhaps, for Hank." Allen took his foot off the fence rail and replaced his hat. "What I wanted to talk to you about was this. I guess you know we've got some races over in Preston next week. They're pretty big, and we get horses from California, Texas, Nevada, Utah, New Mexico and Colorado. That's where Hot Feet won his championship last year. Allen paused. "I was thinking that I might send Hot Feet over to Preston again, and, to make a long story short, *I'd like you to ride him.*"

Allen's last words came forth with a ring. He turned to the boy, smiling, as if to say that all was forgiven, and here was the opportunity to ride a champion in the Southwest's greatest race meeting. His mouth dropped when he saw no elation on the boy's face, only a stiffness that was cold and unchanging.

"It's the chance of a lifetime," Allen added awkwardly. "Last year we had over ten thousand people watching the races. You ride Hot Feet well and you can name your own price in the future . . . not only from me but from other owners who are always looking for good jockeys. Riding race horses is big business, Mac. You can . . ." Allen stopped abruptly. Then he went on. "But maybe you're like me and not interested in the money end of it, Mac. I should have known better than to put it the way I did. Here's what we'll do. I like the way you ride a horse, and the way you handle them. I'll make you my stable partner if you do well with Hot Feet next week. After that, we'll breed our mares to him, and raise our own. You'll own them with me, and do the race riding. How's that for a deal, kid?''

There was still no change in the boy's face.

Allen said, "Hank has been working Hot Feet, so my little champ is just about ready to go. All you'll have to do is ride him around here a few days to get used to his ways. You'll like him, Mac!''

The boy's lips barely moved. "I like him now, but I can't ride him, boss. I can't.'' He saw a sudden change sweep over the man's face. All of Allen's eagerness and enthusiasm were gone. In their place were disappointment and bewilderment. The boy knew he couldn't ride Hot Feet with ten thousand people watching him. He was deathly afraid that just one person among all those thousands would identify him for what he was, a thief, and he would have to run again. He knew, too, that Allen wouldn't force him to ride. It wasn't in this man to think of his riding Hot Feet as anything but a great privilege.

"Have it your own way," Allen said, turning away. The matter was closed. He would never reopen the subject. "If anyone's looking for me, I'll be in town. Back this afternoon," he added brusquely.

The boy crossed the corral to his stallion. The horse put out his tongue for him to pull. This trick had been going on all week long. But it was nothing new to him or the stallion. *When* had it first begun? *Where?*

In Leesburg, the burro Goldie was tied to the rail outside the general store and post office. His eyes were closed and his long ears drooped. He paid no attention to the scrubby Indian ponies hitched to small buckboards and wagons, even when their owners came out of the store and, after loading flour, cloth, potatoes and tin dishes, rattled away. Nor did he hear the loud blare of the juke box coming from the restaurant a few doors down the dirt street.

Finally Gordon emerged from the store, carrying a heavily wrapped package whose weight bent his long, lean body in his effort to hold it. He put it down before Goldie and said, "I'll get a cup of coffee, and then we'll start back. I'm not packing this on you yet, but keep your eyes on it."

Goldie never opened his eyes.

Gordon walked down the street to the restaurant, and went inside. He hoped he could have his coffee in peace, that whoever was putting coins in the juke box would leave. There were several men sitting at the counter. He nodded to them, and was making his way to one of the booths when he saw Cruikshank sitting on the stool at the end of the counter. He nodded to him, and Cruikshank nodded back.

Reaching the booth, he sat down. A newspaper had been left on the seat. He picked it up, noting that it was a Phoenix paper and over a week old. He wasn't interested in the news but turned to the back section, hoping to find a crossword puzzle. His eyes lighted when he saw one.

"What'll you have, Slim?" It was the man from behind the counter.

"Coffee. Maybe a couple of fried eggs, too." Gordon looked up. "Got a pencil on you, Harry?"

"Yeah. Here."

When the waiter had gone, Gordon turned again to the puzzle. While he worked on it he thought of Cruikshank. So Cruikshank was out of jail. Seemed only a few days ago that he'd brought the kid to town and it all had happened. Yet almost a month had passed. Well, he held no grudge against Cruikshank, and Cruikshank was letting him alone. Nothing wrong with that.

His pencil filled the empty squares of the puzzle. They made them too easy. A kid wouldn't have had any trouble doing this one. He wondered how McGregor was making out at the ranch. It'd be nice to get out there, and see him again. He had the time to do it today, but Goldie wouldn't like it. Goldie was used to going straight home from town. And there was the heavy package of magazines to consider. No sense in taking further advantage of Goldie's good nature and willingness to carry his heavy burdens.

It was good of Lew Miller to send him the magazines. There'd be every weekly issue of the *Thoroughbred Record* since the beginning of the year. He'd go through every one of them. Maybe he'd find something that would remind him what it was that made him think he'd seen McGregor's face before.

He finished the puzzle and began running the pencil around its borders. He remembered the blood-stained money in his dresser drawer back home, and his face sobered. He remembered all the kid had said in his delirium when he'd found him. McGregor was convinced he'd been mixed up in a Utah robbery, and that the police were after him. Maybe so. Maybe not. Until the kid got his memory back, he couldn't be sure of anything.

Gordon pressed harder on his pencil, blackening the lines around the puzzle. Besides, what the kid had done or thought he'd done was none of *his* business. He was keeping out of it. All he wanted to do was to find out what made McGregor's face seem so familiar to him. It was a game, more interesting to him than simple crossword puzzles.

He looked up, to find Cruikshank still at the end of the counter, and half-turned in his direction. Everyone else had left the restaurant and the juke box was quiet. The waiter came with his order, and Gordon put down his pencil to eat. But he picked it up again when he'd finished, once more tracing around the puzzle, and thinking of the boy.

He wondered if the kid had regained his memory. Was he still at the ranch or had he decided to move on again? The paper tore beneath his pencil and Gordon turned to the news item above it, tracing the lines around the story as he'd done with the puzzle. It was none of his business what the kid did. He was only interested. If he was going to become involved in other people's affairs, he might as well go back to Hollywood.

Momentarily his pencil stopped on the paper. He found himself reading. His heavy brows lifted as his eyes widened in surprise. For a long while he stared at the story, reading and rereading it. His pencil began moving again, blackening the lines around the story once more.

"Howdy, Slim."

He looked up quickly, pushing the paper to one side. "Hello, Allen," he said.

Allen had a cup of coffee in his hand. He placed it on

the table, and sat down beside Gordon. If he had seen Cruikshank, he gave no indication of it. He drank half his coffee, and then said, "That friend of yours, McGregor, puzzles me, Slim." His narrow brow was furrowed, his eyes on Gordon. "And he gets more puzzling all the time," he added.

Gordon picked up his own cup of coffee, and finished it. He was frightened. "The kid's no friend of mine, Allen. Don't know him at all or anything about him." He didn't want to get mixed up with McGregor. Not after having read the story in the paper at his side.

Allen said, "He was working out pretty well for us until a little over a week ago, when I sent him out to look for a wild stallion thought to be on the upper range. I was afraid for my mares and . . ."

"A wild stallion?" Gordon asked, interested now.

Allen nodded. "You'll have to see him, Slim. He's no mustang but big . . . mighty big."

"Then you got him?"

"We got him all right, but the peculiar part of it is that the kid found him first and didn't let on to us. In fact, we would have turned back and never got him if Hank hadn't been along. Hank knew the kid was lying."

"Strange that he should lie about something like that."

"And peculiar," Allen insisted. "Mighty peculiar. But there's more to it. The kid had gentled this wild outlaw even before we got there. When he knew we had him, he walked right up to the stallion, put a halter on him with no trouble at all, and led him back to the ranch."

"That's hard to believe," Gordon said quietly. "Now and then I've run across a small band of horses on the upper ranges. Nobody could gentle a wild stallion that easily.''

Allen put down his hand flat and hard against the table. ''That's what I think, too. But Hank says that sometimes it happens.''

Gordon shook his head. ''I doubt it,'' he said.

''Come and see for yourself,'' Allen said. ''And here's something that puzzles me more than anything else. This morning I gave the kid the opportunity to ride Hot Feet in next week's races at Preston, and he turned me down! Of course, I could have ordered him to ride, but that's not for me. Here I thought I was giving him a big break and he kicks it aside!'' Allen's puzzlement showed in his face. ''I'd sort of counted on him as my regular rider from the time I took him on. He's a born race rider. Anyone can see that just by the way he sits a horse.''

Gordon's bushy eyebrows were raised again. He glanced away from Allen to the door. He was thinking of the package of *Thoroughbred Records* beside Goldie. ''How *does* he sit a horse, Allen?''

''With short stirrups, but not so short that he loses his balance or control. And forward, and low near the horse's neck. You know how most jocks ride, don't you, Slim? Haven't you ever seen a race, maybe before you came out here?''

Gordon turned back to Allen. ''Yes, I know,'' he said. Then after a long pause he added softly, ''I'd like to talk to the kid.''

''Come along, then. I've got the buckboard outside, and I'll see that you get a ride back to town later.''

Together they left the restaurant.

When they had gone, Cruikshank twisted his gaunt body off the end stool. He walked across to the booth they had left, his large and gloomy eyes on the newspaper that was still there. His worn hands picked it up, and he read the story just above the crossword puzzle, the one marked so heavily in pencil, the story that had brought the startled, frightened look to Gordon's face while he was watching him.

YOUTH WANTED IN UTAH
MURDER SOUGHT HERE

PHOENIX—The search for a boy involved in the robbery of a Salt Lake City diner last month has led to Arizona and is being intensified since the death last week of Henry Clay, the cashier, resulting from injuries suffered during the theft.

All state, county and city police have been alerted, for it is believed the youth will try to cross the border into Mexico. His description is: Between sixteen and eighteen years of age, about five feet five inches tall, red hair, and slight of build.

The three men for whom the boy acted as lookout were captured by police soon after the robbery, and are awaiting trial.

Cruikshank reread the description of the boy, and his eyes were no longer gloomy but shifty and bitter. He knew the reason for Gordon's sudden alarm. *He knew the boy.* His long, bony hands were trembling as he carefully tore the story from the paper, taking part of the crossword puzzle with it. He put it in his pocket. He would have good use for it, but not right now. He was going to wait until he was sure of the best way to use it. He hated them all for what they'd done to him. He hated the sheriff. He hated Gordon. He hated the kid. But most of all he hated Allen, and maybe what he had on the kid would provide him with a way to get at Allen. Mumbling to himself, he left the restaurant.

The torn newspaper lay on the table. The hole left where the clipping had been removed showed part of the next page. Here, too, there was a story concerning a search for a boy. It was only a few lines in length. It was hardly news any longer.

SEARCH ENDS

JACKSON HOLE, WYO., July 25—The search for Alec Ramsay and his famed stallion, the Black, ended today after more than a month of constant but futile search through Wyoming's most primitive and rugged regions. No hope is held for their ever being found alive.

The man from behind the counter went to the table and cleaned it. He took the newspaper, crumpled it, and threw it in with the other trash to be burned.

Black Flame

15

Gordon spoke to Goldie again before climbing into Allen's buckboard. The burro flicked his ears, but otherwise there was no indication that he'd heard. Until he felt the pack on his back his eyes would remain closed.

Taking up the lines of the two horses hitched to the buckboard, Allen said, "No one is going to bother your burro, Slim." Then he laughed, adding, "And it doesn't look like he'll mind waiting a while longer before going home."

Allen backed up the team, turned, and went down the street. They were well outside the town before he spoke again. "I guess I was counting on the kid riding Hot Feet more than I realized. Can't seem to get it off my mind now." Allen paused. "Not that it's terribly important," he went on. "Last year I picked up a race rider over at Preston, and we won all right. It's just that riding Hot

Feet is a pretty personal thing with me. I'd been looking for someone who'd work on the ranch, and then ride for me in the races. Larom is too heavy for race riding. I thought the kid was perfect for the job. I guess I'd thought it all along, that's why his turning me down is hard to take.''

Gordon's eyes didn't leave the team. He thought he knew very well why McGregor didn't want to ride at Preston. McGregor was afraid someone would identify him as the boy wanted by the police. Gordon thought of the news story again. An accomplice in a robbery was one thing, *murder* another. The diner's cashier had died of his injuries. While the kid had been only the lookout, he was still as responsible for the cashier's death as the men who'd been caught.

Gordon shifted uneasily in the hard buckboard seat. He wished he hadn't found that newspaper in the restaurant. Better still, he wished he'd never found McGregor. The last thing he wanted was to become involved in such a mess. But how could he stay out of it now, when he alone knew the whereabouts of someone who was wanted as an accomplice in a murder?

Why was he going to the ranch? Why did he want to talk to McGregor? He wondered what the kid's real name was. Even the police didn't seem to know. It didn't matter, nothing mattered except that he, Gordon, get out of this in some way and still do what he thought was his duty to society. Maybe he expected to talk McGregor into giving himself up to the police. He must have had that in mind when he'd accepted Allen's invitation. If he had intended to inform the authorities of what he knew, he would have gone directly to the sheriff.

"You're pretty quiet, Slim."

"Just thinking," Gordon replied.

"You don't think you could get the kid to ride for me, do you, Slim? After all, he's a friend of yours. He might listen to you."

"He's no friend of mine," Gordon insisted angrily. "I told you I don't know anything about him."

"You don't have to get sore about it," Allen said. "I just figured you might help him change his mind. After all, he was living with you when I hired him."

Gordon didn't look at Allen. "I found him in the desert. He'd been hitchhiking and got lost."

"The desert's a strange place to be hitchhiking," Allen returned. "Lots of strange things about the kid, all right." He clucked to the horses and their hoofs beat faster on the dirt road.

Allen said nothing more, and Gordon was glad of it. He wished someone else would identify the kid so he could stay out of the mess altogether. Not that he wanted to see McGregor go to jail. He liked the kid. If only it hadn't been murder, he might have forgotten the whole thing. Now he had to do something about it. He had to see to it that McGregor was apprehended by the police, and yet stay out of it himself. He wanted none of the publicity he knew would result in the kid's capture. For six years he had lived a peaceful, quiet life. He wanted to keep it that way.

If the kid did ride at Preston, he thought, someone most likely *would* identify him, just as McGregor feared.

Especially if he won, and got his picture in the papers. Wasn't that the answer? He turned to Allen. "Why don't you change your mind and *order* McGregor to ride?"

Allen shook his head adamantly. "No, Slim," he said. "He's got to *want* to ride Hot Feet. That's the only way he'll get up on him now."

A few moments later Allen changed the subject. "Ralph Herbert of the High Crest Ranch in Texas has been after me for months to have a match race at Preston. I bought Hot Feet from him as a weanling, and now that he's a champion Herbert would like to get him back at any price I set. But I'm not selling Hot Feet, and he knows it."

Gordon wasn't listening to Allen. He was trying to figure out a way to get McGregor to ride in the Preston races.

Allen added, "Now Herbert wants a match race between Hot Feet and his horse Night Wind."

Gordon heard this, and turned quickly. "You don't mean the High Crest *thoroughbred*?"

"That's him."

Gordon couldn't help smiling. "You'd be crazy to consent to such a race. Last year Night Wind was voted thoroughbred *Horse-of-the-Year*. He's a great champion, Allen."

"So's Hot Feet," Allen retorted quickly, challengingly. "But how come you know so much about Night Wind?"

"I read about him in some magazines a friend sent me. I used to be quite interested in thoroughbred racing. Night Wind pulled up lame in the Santa Anita Handicap last winter. They found he had torn a ligament so he was unwound and sent home to High Crest Ranch. They hoped to bring him back to racing.''

Allen said, ''You sure know a lot more about him than I do. But maybe it isn't the same horse. Herbert never mentioned anything like that.''

''It's the same horse, if his name is Night Wind and he's a thoroughbred from High Crest Ranch,'' Gordon said quietly.

Allen frowned. ''I know that much is true,'' he replied. Then his face lightened. ''Anyway, Herbert made this proposed match race sound plenty inviting. He wrote that he was sending this thoroughbred, Night Wind, to California, and could very easily ship him via Preston for the races.''

Gordon interrupted, ''Then Night Wind has been put back in training, and is ready to go.''

''Herbert said that match races between thoroughbreds and quarter running horses were rare,'' Allen went on, ''and the crowd at Preston might like to see one. He offered to put up five of his best quarter mares as his end of the purse, if I put up . . .'' Allen stopped.

''If you'd put up what?'' Gordon prompted.

''Hot Feet.''

''You'd lose him, if you did,'' Gordon said. ''Stick to your own kind of racing, and leave the thoroughbreds alone. No quarter horse in the world could stay with Night Wind. Herbert would just like to get Hot Feet from you the easiest possible way . . . and such a match race would be it.''

"I'd like to get those mares," Allen said thoughtfully. "I sure would. High Crest Ranch is such a big operation that Herbert's cornered the finest quarter-horse stock in the country."

"And some of the best thoroughbred blood, too," Gordon added. "That's exactly why you should stick to quarter-horse racing, Allen."

"Oh, I'm going to stick to it, all right. That's why I'd like to get hold of those High Crest mares. But I'm not racing Hot Feet against Night Wind the way Herbert wants it. I've written him I'd race Hot Feet any day of the week against his Night Wind at three hundred yards but no farther. He wants the race over a quarter of a mile. I'm not that dumb. Hot Feet's best distance is three hundred. I'd be taking too big a chance racing him at a quarter."

"You'd be taking a big chance at any distance," Gordon said.

"No," Allen insisted. "Hot Feet could beat anything Herbert has at three hundred yards, and I'd take his mares."

The ranch was less than a mile away. At the far-off sound of running hoofs they turned to look across the plateau. Allen's face disclosed his alarm at sight of the running black horse. For a moment he thought the big stallion had broken from his corral and was free. Then he saw the slight figure on the horse's back and, realizing it had to be McGregor, his fear left him. In its place came swift anger. McGregor had no right to take the black horse from the corral without his permission!

"Say, that horse out there is beginning to move!" Gordon exclaimed.

"That's the outlaw I told you about," Allen returned. "The one we caught."

Gordon looked at Allen, but it was only a fleeting glance. He couldn't keep his eyes off the fast approaching horse. "And that's McGregor riding him?"

"No one else would be up on him," Allen said brusquely. "He's got no business being out there, running him like that."

"Open your eyes, Allen. You've never seen such strides! And the kid's making him go. *Look at them come!*"

But Allen's gaze had left the black stallion. At the far side of a group of steers he saw Hank Larom riding Hot Feet. Larom turned Hot Feet around as he neared the path of the boy and horse. He was going to make a race of it! Hot Feet was given his head as the black stallion came rushing up from behind.

Allen took a quick breath at Hot Feet's fast start. He knew no horse in the world could reach his top speed faster than Hot Feet. His champion was in full stride almost at once, and the distance between the two horses remained the same. *Nothing could catch Hot Feet now* . . . for three hundred yards no horse could beat him! After that distance, Allen decided, it didn't matter if the black horse did overtake Hot Feet.

For almost the full three hundred yards there was no change in the position of the racing horses. Allen's eyes blazed more brightly than ever in his love for his horse.

He told himself that the black stallion could run, there was no doubt of it. But Hot Feet was running under saddle and carrying Larom's heavy weight. The black horse was being ridden bareback by a lightly built kid. Allen banged his fist against the buckboard. "Come on, you little horse! Move away from him! Move!"

They heard a short blast from the black stallion, echoed by the boy's shrill call. They saw McGregor bend closer to the stallion's neck, and then with startling suddenness the horse came on with terrifying speed. The blazing light in Allen's eyes flickered and died.

If the black stallion had been running before, he was flying now! It was as though in one mighty leap he had overtaken Hot Feet. He became nothing but a black, whirling blur in the watchers' eyes. They couldn't make out the boy on his back, for he was one with the horse. Faster and faster he came toward them, his strides lengthening more and more. They knew they had never seen a horse run like this. He was like nothing real. This was no horse, there was no rider . . . nothing but a blackness moving across the plateau with electrifying speed. It whipped past them, low and long, and the air twisted about them. The team screamed and rose in their harness. The swirling dust moved away, going faster and faster, and only the beat of magnificent strides betrayed it for what it was. Gordon and Allen watched and watched until the black stallion disappeared behind the distant barns.

Their gazes were still turned in his direction when Larom rode Hot Feet up beside the buckboard. His face was stiff and pale. "Boss, did you see him! I ain't never seen a horse run like that. Boss, he was flyin'!"

Allen turned to Larom, and then to the sweated, snorting Hot Feet. He felt his anger quickly return. His mouth twitched as to himself he cursed the black stallion. Aloud he said, "Take Hot Feet back to the corral, Hank."

Allen picked up the long lines to the team. Before the buckboard moved Gordon said, "That black stallion only started to run when he passed Hot Feet."

Allen clucked to the horses. "Nothing can beat Hot Feet at three hundred yards . . . nothing. I'll bet he had the black stallion beaten at that distance, close to three hundred yards anyway, and he was carrying a lot more weight. It would be a different story if he'd been going light."

"Have it your way," Gordon said agreeably. "But I was thinking of something else. Do you still want those High Crest mares?"

"You trying to be funny, Slim?"

"No. Herbert wants the match race at more than three hundred yards, doesn't he?"

"I told you all that. That's why there's not going to be any match race." He turned to Gordon. "What the devil are you driving at, Slim?"

"The kid could really set things afire riding that black stallion in a distance race . . . the longer the better, I think."

Allen said nothing. His eyes lost some of their anger, and became more thoughtful. "You mean . . ."

"I mean here's your chance to pick up the mares you

want. Let Herbert select any distance he likes for the race.''

''Race the black stallion, instead of Hot Feet, against Night Wind?'' Allen knew Gordon meant exactly that. He wanted only to hear himself say it, to see how it sounded, to see if it made any sense to him.

''Herbert would think you were crazy for suggesting such a race, and that would give you a chance to set up 'most anything you want in the way of an additional purse.'' Gordon paused. ''Maybe a few more mares,'' he suggested cagily.

''He'd think I was crazy, all right,'' Allen said slowly. ''And I sure would be.'' He added quickly, ''No, Slim. Racing a wild horse isn't in my line.''

In the distance they saw the black stallion again. McGregor had taken him from behind the barns, and was moving him back down the plain. Allen's gaze never left the horse and rider. He watched the easy, unhurried movements of the stallion. McGregor wasn't pushing the horse now. Allen thought again of Gordon's suggestion, and his face became dark and troubled by the conflicting emotions that surged within him. He wanted those High Crest quarter mares. He'd like to beat Herbert at his own game. *But to race a wild range horse at Preston was unthinkable!* He was as silly as Slim even to be considering it.

Gordon was saying something, but Allen didn't listen to him. Instead he watched the stallion's strides lengthen. McGregor was sitting almost upright, trying to hold down the horse's speed. But suddenly the kid gave in to the stallion's demand to run again. He had moved forward, and was almost lost from sight by the horse's whipping mane. Allen saw them pass the chuck wagon he kept on the range, and his eyes left the horse for a fleeting second to glance at his wrist watch. If McGregor took the stallion straight down the plain they would pass an empty corral which, Allen knew, was a little over a quarter of a mile from the chuck wagon. It would give him a better idea of how fast this horse was running.

When Gordon saw Allen glance at his wrist watch, he knew the rancher was clocking the stallion, so he said nothing more. His arguments in favor of racing the black horse at Preston were no longer needed. Allen's watch, during the next few seconds, was all that was necessary. Gordon's gaze remained on Allen until the rancher turned to look at his watch again. Gordon saw the incredulous look that came quickly to Allen's face when he noted the time made by the running horse.

They had reached the ranch before Allen spoke again. "I've been sort of mulling over what you suggested back there," he said slowly.

"Yes?" Gordon waited, but he knew what was coming.

"Do you honestly think that black horse could beat a thoroughbred, one as good as you said Night Wind is?" Allen asked. His watch had told him no quarter horse in the world could have run faster over a quarter-mile than had the stallion. But he knew nothing about thoroughbred records.

"The way he ran today he could beat *anything*," Gordon said. "I'd stake all I have on it."

Allen climbed down from the buckboard. "Well, I might just think a little more about it, Slim." Then he added, hastily, "Mind you now, I'm not saying I'm going to do it."

"No, of course not," Gordon said, but he had no doubt that the match race would be arranged.

Allen spoke again, and his voice held a ring of excitement that couldn't be completely muted. "Even if I *did* decide to do it, maybe the kid won't want to ride in the race," he said.

Gordon replied, "You could *order* him to ride. It wouldn't be the same as the way you feel about his riding Hot Feet."

"Yeah, I suppose I could do that," Allen said thoughtfully. "Well, no sense talking any more about it, Slim. Come in the house, and wait there for the kid to get back."

"I've changed my mind," Gordon said. "I'll see him some other time. If you've got anyone around to drive me back to town, I'd like to go now."

Allen shook his head. "Sure, I got someone, but you said . . ."

"I know what I said, but it can wait now," Gordon interrupted. "I'll see McGregor on my next trip to town." Everything had been arranged so perfectly that he could afford to wait now. He was almost certain that Allen would decide in favor of the match race, and that McGregor would be forced to ride at Preston. There, someone would identify him as the boy wanted by the police.

"You're a strange fellow, Slim," Allen said thoughtfully. "First you want to talk to McGregor, and then you don't. You like horses and racing, yet you got only a burro for yourself. You seem to be interested in folks, and yet you shut yourself up in the pines, and most of the time see no one. Maybe you're not a happy guy, Slim."

"You're wrong, Allen. Most of the time I'm very happy. It's only once in a while that I feel I've let myself down and others as well." He turned to take another look at the distant horse and rider. "This is just one of those times," he added quietly. "I'll get over it."

Race Rider

16

After Gordon had left, Allen waited impatiently for McGregor, who had the horse in a walk, and was slowly approaching the corral. Allen had decided to race the black horse at Preston, providing he could get the kid to ride him. Allen moved toward the boy and horse. He hoped he wasn't going to run into any trouble with McGregor. His best way of avoiding it was by getting right to the point. He wasn't going to *ask* McGregor to ride. It would be an order. He wasn't going to take any more disobedience from McGregor.

Allen saw the uneasiness in the boy's flushed face at his approach. McGregor expected a reprimand for taking the horse from the corral, but instead Allen said, "Take him in, and wash him down good, McGregor."

"Yes, sir."

"And you're riding at Preston," Allen added quickly. "But it's not going to be on Hot Feet. You'll be up on this horse, racing him like you just showed me he can run." He paused, his eyes unwavering. "That's an order. If you don't like it, I'm firing you now. So make up your mind quick!"

The boy's face showed white beneath his tan. He said nothing.

"Well, McGregor?" Allen waited, his feet beginning to shift uneasily, for seldom had he used such tactics in getting cooperation from his men. Yet he felt it was the only way to handle McGregor. "You win with him," he continued less harshly, "and maybe we can discuss again what we talked about this morning. Maybe he'll be *yours* in a short while. But I'm not promising anything. I'm just telling you to ride him in the race or leave the ranch today. Understand, McGregor?"

Finally the boy nodded. "I'll stay, and ride him," he said, ". . . at Preston."

Allen's face softened. "That's more like it," he said. "Now cool him off, and take care of him, Mac. He's got a big job to do next week."

"Yes, sir," the boy answered tonelessly. He rode the stallion toward the corral.

Allen hurried into the house. Entering the dining room, he made his way around a long table covered with red-checkered tablecloths. Through the kitchen door, at the far end of the room, came the rattling of pots and pans. He went to the doorway. At the kitchen table stood Reni, the ranch cook, his hands in flour, and his watery blue eyes on the pan in front of him. Allen said, "I'll be using the phone a few minutes, Ren."

He closed the kitchen door, and went to the telephone in the corner of the dining room. He preferred not to have Reni overhear his conversation. No sense in having everybody know what he intended to propose to Herbert . . . not right now, anyway.

He cranked the wall telephone, and waited for the Leesburg operator to answer. After a few seconds she said, "Yes, Mr. Allen."

"Elsie, I want to put in a long distance call to Texas. . . . Yes, you heard me right, Elsie, I said Texas. What was that? . . . I know it's a long way off. . . . What was that? . . . Oh, yes, I'm sorry, Elsie. I want the High Crest Ranch near Abilene. I want to speak to Mr. Ralph Herbert. . . . Yes, that's right. Ralph Herbert at the High Crest Ranch. You got it now, Elsie? I'll wait. You go right ahead. . . . Of course I'll wait, Elsie. . . . No, I don't care how long it'll take. . . . No, Elsie. I'll wait. Please put the call through. Thank you, Elsie."

He leaned against the wall and looked out the window. He could see the vast plateau stretched endlessly before him and, to his right, the mountain range with its peaks golden against the purple-blue sky. He heard the bellowing of the cattle in the distance, and then, close to the ranch, came the beat of hoofs. He turned in the direction of the corral and saw the black stallion moving about. A moment later he saw McGregor go to him, carrying a bucket of water. Allen shook his head in wonder as the stallion trotted toward the boy without hesitation and shoved his muzzle into the pail. It was too easy for McGregor. Everything had been too easy. After all, the black stallion had been an outlaw until a little over a week ago. Allen continued to watch them. He *had* to accept this strange, unnatural relationship, but he sure didn't understand it.

"Hello. Hello. High Crest Ranch? Is this Ralph Herbert? . . . Ralph, this is Allen, Irv Allen up near Preston. . . . Fine. Fine. How are you? . . . Good, glad to hear it, Ralph. . . . Yes, we'll be there on Saturday. How about you, Ralph? Are you coming? Good. Great. . . . No, I haven't changed my mind, Ralph. Three hundred yards is the only distance I'll race Hot Feet, this year anyway. . . . No, a quarter of a mile is too far for him. He can't hold his speed that long. I might as well admit. . . . What's that, Ralph? . . . Yes, I know a quarter is pretty short for a thoroughbred, or at least I've been told so. Don't know much about that breed of horse, as you're aware. . . . I guess the match race is out, Ralph. . . . Yes, it *is* too bad. I know how the crowd would like it. . . . Sure, Ralph, I know. Well, I guess that's about all. I just wanted to make sure you knew the match race with Hot Feet couldn't possibly be run under the conditions you've set for it."

Allen's eyes shifted to the window while he listened to Herbert continue to talk about the appeal such a race would have for the crowd at Preston. Finally he said, "Well, I'll see you Saturday then, Ralph." He waited until Herbert was ready to hang up. He tried to keep the eagerness out of his voice when he said, "Oh, Ralph . . .

something's come up here that just might appeal to you, and then again it might not. The boys picked up a wild horse on the upper range awhile back. . . . Yeah, that's what I said. . . . No, he's not the mustang type, a little bigger and racier. We've grown pretty fond of him. Spent a lot of time grooming him and so on. We like the way he runs, but since he's not a registered horse we can't race him at Preston. I thought that maybe you'd have something to match against him.''

There was a long pause at the other end. Finally Allen heard Herbert's voice again. He listened, and then said, ''Well, Night Wind seems a little hard to take, Ralph. After all, this is a horse we just picked up on the range. . . . Yeah, I know Night Wind is the *only* thoroughbred you're able to get to Preston. . . . Sure, I know that a thoroughbred racing one of our local horses is what would appeal to the crowd. But, Ralph . . . Sure, Ralph . . . Yeah, I know, Ralph.''

Herbert was talking rapidly, insistently. Allen let him go on for a long time before saying, ''Well, all right, Ralph. I guess we can work it out. Shall we make the race over a quarter of a mile then? . . . Sure, that's fine, Ralph. You'll put up five quarter mares as your end of the purse and I'll put up Hot Feet. I'd sure hate to lose my little horse, Ralph, but I don't think I will. This black horse is pretty fast as horses go around these parts. . . . Sure, Ralph, I know you'd hate to lose your quarter mares, too. Well, it's all in the game, heh? . . . Oh, Ralph, I just had a thought. This new horse of ours seems to like distance. You know how those range horses are, plenty of stamina. Would you be interested in making the race, say, maybe a mile instead of a quarter?''

He smiled at the eagerness of the voice at the other end of the line. He listened for a while, and then said, ''Oh, you needn't put up *ten* mares just because you like the idea so much, Ralph. Five mares are plenty. . . . Well, okay, Ralph, if you insist. I know you only expected a quarter-mile race, and your Night Wind is better over a longer distance. You told me that once before, Ralph. . . . Yes. Sure, Ralph. No, I won't go back on my word. We'll be there Saturday. . . . Yeah, I'll tell the race officials at Preston. I'll get in touch with them right away, so they can put it on the program. . . . What's that, Ralph? . . . Sure, I'll agree to that. *If either horse, yours or mine, fails to show up at the post it'll be the same as losing the race, and the other will take the purse. . . .* Sure, Ralph. Sounds fair to me, too. Okay . . . right you are. . . . Sure, Ralph. . . . So long, Ralph.'' He hung up the receiver, and sat down, breathing hard. *Ten mares from High Crest Ranch!* More, much more, than he'd hoped for. He began making plans for them.

In Leesburg, Elsie, the operator, pulled out the switchboard plug to the Allen ranch, and then removed her headset. No other lights flashed on the small board. She leaned toward the open window facing the street, and the stool creaked beneath her ponderous weight. She saw her friend Janie Conover walking by, and called. They put their heads together for a few minutes, and then Janie went bustling down the street. Elsie looked around for someone else who would be interested in learning what was going to happen at the Preston races on Saturday.

Gordon had finished packing the magazines on Goldie when the news reached him. A saggy, medium-sized man sporting a droopy, full-mouthed mustache came out of the general store.

"Slim, y'heard about it?"

"Heard what, Gus?"

"Allen's gonna' race that wild hoss he's got against some Texas thoroughbred this Satidy at Preston. For the purse he's puttin' up Hot Feet against ten mares from the Texas feller. Ain't no backin' down by either of 'em, either. Got to show up an' race or else they lose. Whatya think o' that, Slim? Allen puttin' up Hot Feet like he's doin', an' racin' a wild range hoss?"

Gordon turned to Goldie. "I think," he said, "that it's time we were going home," and he led Goldie down the street. He didn't want to return to Leesburg until it was all over. He realized what the coming race would mean to McGregor, Allen, and everybody else concerned. A bombshell exploding in their midst would be nothing compared with the shock that would rock the racing world if a captured outlaw stallion beat Night Wind, thoroughbred Horse-of-the-Year. The kid had no idea what he was getting into. Neither did Allen. They'd be overwhelmed by publicity. And for McGregor it would mean the end of his running away from the police. As for himself, well, he was out of it now. He wouldn't become involved in this very messy business. He had instigated the race, making possible McGregor's capture. Yet he was out of it completely. He hoped that in time he'd be able to forget what he'd done to the kid.

Gus ran past, and Gordon saw him stop to tell the news to Cruikshank, who was sitting on the steps of the café. As Gordon went by, he noticed that Cruikshank was showing great interest in Gus's story. There was even a trace of a smile on Cruikshank's thin lips. Gordon left town, knowing Cruikshank would enjoy nothing more than to have Allen lose the race and his prized Hot Feet. But the black stallion wouldn't be beaten, not if the kid was able to ride him as he had ridden him today.

Cruikshank continued sitting on the steps of the café for a long while. His big hands worked nervously up and down his thighs, wiping off the sweat on them. He'd heard about the black stallion at the Allen ranch, and knew that only the kid was able to handle him. Soon he'd tell the sheriff who the kid was. But not now. He'd wait until Saturday. He'd wait until just before the race. With no kid to ride the stallion, there'd be no race. And Allen would lose Hot Feet, his cherished possession.

Back at the ranch, McGregor stayed with his horse, moving with him about the corral, finding solace in his very nearness. Often he just watched the stallion standing so still in the sun, his black coat shining as though afire. His stallion was no wild horse, no mustang who had spent years roaming endless ranges. Every inch of him denoted his fine blood and breeding . . . the small head, the great eyes and body. His every move disclosed it.

He rubbed the stallion's neck. Riding him today had been like riding the wind! The black stallion had passed

Hot Feet as though the bay horse had been standing still. He had been called upon to run, and he had flown, snorting, wanting to fight as he had drawn close to Hot Feet. McGregor had called in his ear and the stallion had responded, leaving Hot Feet alone, and running the way the boy had wanted him to run. McGregor knew he could handle this stallion, *his* stallion. He knew this much but no more. He couldn't remember when or where it had all started. But soon he would know. Every day he came a little closer to knowing, to remembering.

He ran his hands down one of the stallion's long legs, and lifted a hoof. He began cleaning it. Every small job was familiar, and brought him that much closer to remembering. He would put shoes on his stallion for the race. He wouldn't have any trouble. He'd done it before.

There were moments when he found himself looking forward to racing this horse. He couldn't understand why. But he didn't attempt to fight it. He accepted his mounting excitement, the compelling urge to race. He knew that he had not felt this way when Allen had asked him to ride Hot Feet. Why was racing his black horse so different? Why did just the thought of it sometimes send his blood rushing, driving the very dangers of the race away from him?

Yet there were other moments when he felt fear and panic take over his body, when he thought of running away. But he realized he couldn't leave his horse now. Finally he came to a decision. He would tell Allen that he and the stallion should be kept away from all the horses and people at Preston until the race was called. Otherwise he wouldn't be responsible for what the stallion might do. Allen would understand and agree. His stake in the match race was too high for him not to go along with anything McGregor might propose in the best interests of the stallion.

Actually, it was only what might happen after the race that McGregor feared. He tried to convince himself that there was a good chance nobody would be able to identify him in Allen's racing silks. And he'd leave the track right after the race. He'd get the stallion to act up and no one would come very close to them. They'd return to the ranch, and someday soon, if Allen had meant what he'd said, the stallion would be his!

He finished cleaning the perfect hoofs. He started toward the corral fence and found the black horse following him. He stopped, and then walked on again. He heard the stallion behind him. Once more he stopped, this time to turn and go back to him, pressing his head against the black neck.

Lightening Shadows

17

The following days were unlike any that had gone before. There wasn't a man on the ranch who didn't know of Saturday's match race and the conditions under which it would be run. They gave any excuse to get near the black stallion's corral. In large groups they watched him, accepting him for what he was, a wild stallion, a beautiful stallion, but never broken, not ready to carry Allen's racing colors at Preston.

But Allen never asked their opinions, and his grim face deterred them from offering voluntary advice. He realized he had not been successful in keeping anything from anybody. He supposed that Elsie had given him away, and regretted that he hadn't been mindful of her listening to his conversation with Herbert at the time. However, it made no great difference. It was only an annoyance. He didn't like the looks of skepticism on the faces of his men.

Now that he had committed himself to the match race, he watched over the boy and the black stallion more than ever, worrying about them. These last few days were serious business. Nothing must happen to either of them. The kid had his own peculiar ideas about Saturday's race, and Allen had agreed to them readily. There was too much at stake to do otherwise. At McGregor's suggestion, they would van the stallion to Preston the night before the race rather than a day early, as he'd intended to do. They would park the van in the outlying district of the track and keep the stallion there until the race was called. All this was to prevent him from becoming over-excited by the presence of other horses and the crowd.

Perhaps McGregor's ideas weren't so peculiar at that, for they were racing a stallion who only a short time ago had been running wild. Yet it was hard for Allen to think of this horse as being wild and unbroken, as his men did. He had spent too many hours watching the boy handle him with an ease that made every horse on the place, including Hot Feet, seem much more wild. But he mustn't forget that the black stallion accepted only the boy, that no one else could get near him, much less ride him. If anything happened to McGregor, handling the stallion would be a far different story.

Early Friday morning they rode to the north of the ranch where there was no grass, only hard-packed sand. Here they had laid out a mile course, and the black stallion had been trained before the eyes of just two spectators, Allen and Larom.

For this last gallop at the ranch, McGregor took the great stallion far beyond the starting mark. He kept him at a lope, waiting for him to get warm. His own blood became heated at the feel of the reins and the creaking of saddle leather. He rose in his stirrups and the irons felt worn and familiar on the balls of his feet. With a loose rein, he held the stallion down to a lope by his voice alone. He never worried him. He looked between the small, pricked ears at the hills in the distance. He felt a strong urge to let the stallion go on, never to turn back. No one would catch them! They would go to the hills, and then turn to the western range. They would climb, and then descend into that vast, unknown country of the great canyons. No one would find them there.

He spoke to his horse, and turned him in a wide circle, still loping. He saw Allen and Larom two miles away, waiting for them to come down. He guided the stallion toward them. What would he gain by taking his horse into the desolate canyon country? Freedom for a while, but certain death in the end. For just as it was true that no one would find them, he would not be able to find his way out. It was far better to stay here, to take a chance that the race would come and go without his being caught by the police. Only Gordon was aware of the crime he had committed, and Gordon was keeping quiet.

He moved forward a little more, and the stallion responded with longer strides. He thought of the race to come against Night Wind. Why did that name seem so familiar? Had he known Night Wind? Had he ridden Night Wind just as he was now riding the black stallion? Had he once been a jockey? He must have been, for there was nothing strange about this racing bridle and saddle. How long ago and where? And why had he been in Salt Lake City? Why had he regained consciousness in the back of a trailer truck? He remembered the money Gordon was keeping for him, and it was easy to figure out the answers. He had been a jockey. He had run out of money. He had helped some men rob a diner. He had been in a fight. He had succeeded in getting away by hopping a truck.

He clucked to the stallion and sat down to ride. He felt the slight twinge of head pain, the first in more than a week. He had thought himself completely well except for not being able to remember. But he wasn't. The pain had returned.

The stallion snorted, and showed fight, but there was no slackening of stride. The boy looked ahead and saw Larom already on the course with Hot Feet. For the past few days Hot Feet had acted as the stallion's prompter. Hot Feet was taken to the last three hundred yards of the mile course, and never asked to run all out. It had been Allen's idea. He wanted to use Hot Feet but didn't care to have him race the black stallion even at three hundred yards. He didn't want to be convinced of the black stallion's superior speed at so short a distance.

Larom allowed Allen this indulgence by never admitting Hot Feet was going all out when the black stallion passed them. But Larom knew, as did McGregor, that

Hot Feet could not stay within the stallion's shadow at *any* distance.

Today was no exception. The boy gave the stallion his head at the start of the mile course. He felt the sudden release of powerful muscles. He heard the stallion's furious snorts at just the sight of Hot Feet running far ahead of him. McGregor bent low against the straining neck and called repeatedly, knowing that only the sound of his voice would remind the stallion of the boy who was riding him.

The black horse was in full stride now, and he closed the distance to Hot Feet in electrifying seconds. Reaching Hot Feet's hindquarters, his strides shortened. The boy spoke to him, and he went on, leaving Hot Feet behind as if the small bay horse had come to a sudden, full stop.

McGregor rode him out for another mile, and then trotted him back to where Larom was standing. The ranch foreman watched every movement of the stallion, and finally he said, "Nothing could have beaten him today."

"If he runs that way tomorrow," McGregor began, "we'll . . ."

"*When* he runs that way tomorrow, y'mean," Larom interrupted. "It ain't goin' to be any other way ever, not as long as you're up on him. He *wants* to run for you. Ain't no doubt about that. He's a killer, an outlaw. . . . Everything he does shows that. But he'll do what you want, because you ask him to do it. Jus' look how you got him under saddle the other day. Never a fight, nothin'. He jus' took it 'cause you asked him. I've seen horses take a likin' to certain people before, but nothin' ever like this.''

McGregor touched his horse, and the stallion moved in quick, springy strides to the front of Hot Feet. How could he tell Larom that this was no outlaw horse he rode? How could he explain to him that this stallion had worn saddle and bridle before, and that he had ridden him before?

From behind him came the man's voice again. "I wouldn't miss tomorrow's race for the whole state of Arizona. Ain't goin' to be nothin' like it again, not once they see what you and him do to that track. I guess I'd give up anything, if I had to, jus' to see it.''

McGregor said nothing. He felt the same way. He knew it was more than Allen's orders that was taking him to Preston to ride. He *wanted* to race the stallion. He was excited about it. He was a fool. He might be giving up everything, including his freedom.

Late that same afternoon, Allen drove the van to the corral where the boy and stallion awaited him. It was a large van with room for six horses. Allen had bought it when he had purchased his broodmares a year ago. Now it was to carry the black stallion to Preston.

Only a few riders had been able to come off the range to watch the loading. The others would start for Preston later that night. Larom waved the riders back from the barred gate. He waited until Allen had the van's side door opposite the gate, and then took down the bars.

In the center of the corral, McGregor held his horse. He waited for them to lower the van's ramp, to adjust the heavy fiber matting, and then he led his horse toward it.

He knew he wasn't going to have any trouble loading him. He knew Allen and Larom would shake their heads at the wonder of it all, just as they had done when he'd thrown Allen's maroon racing blanket over the stallion without any trouble, without a restless movement from the horse. They should have known then that there was no magic about it, that he'd done all this many times before to the same horse . . . somewhere, long ago.

Larom was standing on one side of the ramp, and Allen on the other. Neither wanted to allow the stallion to get through the openings there. They expected trouble. Seeing them, the stallion shied, moving with marvelous ease and swiftness.

"Move away from the ramp," McGregor told them.

Reluctantly, and afraid of what might happen, they moved to the sides of the corral. The boy went forward then, the stallion following on a slack lead rope. McGregor walked up the ramp without turning around, but he knew his horse was right behind him. He heard the light hoofs come down on the matting calmly and deliberately, as he had expected. Yet the sound of them, and the closeness of the stallion's blanketed body once they were inside the van, caused his head to pound. He raised a hand to his forehead. *Where* had this all happened before? He was so close to remembering!

As he turned his horse around and backed him into the straight stall at the front of the van, his head pounded even more. *A narrow, straight stall. A stallion crosstied. A great roar, a drone of engines.* All these he could remember. Not so long ago. He closed his eyes. He waited. He prayed for it all to come back to him.

"Set, Mac?"

He opened his eyes. Larom was standing in the door-way. The starter ground. The engine caught, steadied, idled.

Larom said, "I'd better ride up with the boss. He's so jittery I ain't trustin' his drivin' over the mountains."

The door closed. He was alone again. He could wait. He had time. It would be five hours before they reached Preston. So much could happen to him in five hours. He might be able to remember *everything* in five hours. He turned to the stallion, wanting his help more than ever before.

The van moved down the dirt road toward Leesburg and the mountain range beyond.

That evening Gordon sat down and reached again for the stack of *Thoroughbred Records* on the table beside him. He wasn't looking for a picture of McGregor. He was trying to forget McGregor and was being more successful than he'd hoped. He'd found the contents of the magazine more interesting than he'd remembered. He made a mental note to subscribe to the *Thoroughbred Record*. It wouldn't disrupt his quiet life to keep up with what was going on in the racing world.

He hadn't riffled the pages of all the issues looking for a picture of McGregor. He had convinced himself that it wouldn't matter much if he *did* find McGregor's picture in the magazine. So the kid had been a jockey. A jockey turned thief and murder accomplice. Finding his picture would mean only that he would know McGregor's real name. So he had decided to proceed in his usual, orderly way, and begin at the beginning. He had spent the first night reading every word of the January 1st issue, and the second night the following week's issue. Tonight the issue of January 15th lay on his lap.

This procedure, he thought, would give him a complete picture of what had happened in racing this year. He would go along with the thoroughbreds from week to week, coming to the big races in their proper sequence. It would be almost as good as though he had attended them. He would never cheat by skipping issues to learn who had won the Kentucky Derby, the Preakness, the Belmont, and other classics.

This way, too, he told himself, would help him to forget McGregor and what he'd done to the kid. But tomorrow, he realized, would be the worst time of all for him. Tomorrow the kid would race, and his running from the police would come to an end.

He picked up the magazine from his lap. He studied the cover, driving his disciplined mind to note every muscle of the thoroughbred horse pictured there. It was a dark stallion, wearing racing bridle but no saddle. He was solid, good-looking. He seemed to be a big horse, standing perhaps over sixteen hands. The bridle reins hung loosely over his thick neck and crest. He had good eyes and a wide, intelligent head. A white stripe ran from forehead to muzzle, and there was white on all four legs, adding emphasis to his dark body. He had sloping shoulders, powerful hind muscles, and low-set hocks. He was a very racy type. He was all thoroughbred.

It was not until Gordon read the print at the bottom of the cover that he realized he was looking at a picture of Night Wind. The caption read, "Night Wind—He'll Be Back."

Gordon's long, thin fingers pressed deeply into the magazine until the whites of his nails showed. Finally he turned over the cover. It was no time to be reminded of Night Wind. Yet when he came to the story inside regarding *The Cover Horse* he read it quickly as though to get it over with and then forget about it.

Night Wind, voted Horse-of-the-Year, is recovering satisfactorily from an injury suffered at Santa Anita. He is at the High Crest Ranch in Texas, and his owner, Ralph Herbert, expects to have him back at the ranch track by spring. If he trains well he'll be sent to California sometime during the summer months for another campaign.

Night Wind is a five-year-old son of Count Fleet-Lovely Lady by Sir Galahad III. He was bred by his owner, Ralph Herbert. He is trained by . . .

Gordon turned the page. He had had enough of Night Wind for tonight, *tonight of all nights!* A large advertisement caught his attention, and his sunbleached, heavy eyebrows came up quickly as he read the headline: "His Daughter Won the Kentucky Derby BUT His Fee Still Remains at $500!" Beneath it was a picture of a black horse, *the black horse he had seen at Allen's ranch!*

Still holding the magazine, Gordon got to his feet, trying to control the trembling of his hands. He told

himself that the resemblance between the two stallions
was remarkable, but it didn't necessarily mean they were
one and the same horse! This picture was of the Black,
one of the foremost sires in the country—sire of Black
Minx, the filly who had won the Kentucky Derby, and
sire of Satan, a world's champion before his retirement!

He looked again at the picture, his bright eyes missing
nothing. He remembered the black horse at Allen's, and
compared the two stallions. The heads were surely the
same . . . small, noble and arrogant. Yes, and the eyes,
too . . . very large and set wide apart. Ears were the
very same. And their bodies were alike in every detail.

He couldn't sit down. He tried to remember clearly the
black stallion he had seen McGregor riding. He saw him
again, coming toward him, his body low, and head held
high. . . . That long and slender neck arched even at full
gallop. . . . The long mane so heavy yet windblown in his
great speed.

He turned again to the photograph. One horse was a
famous sire and the other a wild stallion. Yet they were so
much alike in every respect!

Gordon's face, weathered by years spent in the sun,
turned somewhat pale. They *could* be one and the same
horse, *but they weren't, of course.* He was crazy even to
consider it. One horse was at the famous stock farm
operated by Alec Ramsay and Henry Dailey. It said so
right in the advertisement. The Black was in New York
State, close to three thousand miles away. The other
horse was in Preston, awaiting tomorrow's race with
Night Wind.

Gordon sat down in his chair again, and gradually the color came back to his face. He even smiled a little. He was trying to laugh at himself. Finally he was able to turn the page. He began reading an article written by a veterinarian on the proper care of foaling mares.

His eyes followed the type, but his mind refused to concentrate on the article. He remembered Allen telling him about the strange, almost uncanny relationship between the outlaw stallion and McGregor. The kid had been able to handle the horse from the very beginning, putting a halter on him, leading him back to the ranch, and shortly thereafter riding him. Gordon remembered replying to Allen that this was all very hard for him to believe. He had gone to the ranch to see for himself. He had found everything just as Allen had said he would. He, too, had accepted the strange relationship between the boy and the stallion. There had been no alternative. *But now?*

His lean body shifted uneasily in the deep chair. Now, if he looked at it this way, if he told himself that the horse was no wild stallion, that he had been broken and ridden before, could the horse then be . . . It was hard for him to say *the Black*. It was too ridiculous!

Nevertheless, Gordon found himself turning back again and again to the picture of the famous black sire. At last he got to his feet, angrily throwing the magazine to the floor. He went to the other issues on the table, the issues so neatly arranged in their proper weekly sequence. He riffled the pages of each one, his eyes scanning only the headlines. He did not really expect to find anything, yet he couldn't stop looking.

When he came to the issue for the third week of June he grabbed it, but didn't throw it on the floor with the others. Nor did he open the magazine. It wasn't necessary. On the cover was a picture of *McGregor* standing beside his *"wild" stallion!* Only the caption didn't say this. Instead it read: "Alec Ramsay and the Black—Lost in Wyoming Wilderness."

Gordon's knees buckled, and he caught himself on the arm of his chair. He lowered himself to the seat, and turned to the story inside. He learned of the plane's forced landing, and the vigorous search the first few days for the Black and Alec Ramsay. He picked up the following week's issue, and read of more days of constant search through miles of desolate wilderness. He read one issue after another, the stories of the search becoming shorter, and telling of gradually diminishing hope. The last issue stated that the search had ended and that all hope of finding Alec Ramsay and the Black, dead or alive, had ended as well.

Gordon staggered to his feet. He went to the closet, and got his jacket and hat. By starting now he'd be in Leesburg early tomorrow morning. He'd borrow a car, and get to Preston shortly after noon. He must tell McGregor who he was, and that he had nothing to fear from the police. *McGregor was Alec Ramsay!*

Gordon went out the door, shouting excitedly, "Goldie! Goldie!" He was running through the darkness when the thought came to him that Alec Ramsay didn't realize he was riding the Black! No one knew this but himself! Maybe he wouldn't be able to get there before the match race. *The Black racing Night Wind.* The Black coming back to the races *in Preston.* He couldn't miss it! No one who liked to see a horse run would want to miss it. Yet there would be only a small number of people watching, and none would know they were witnessing a sight many thousands of others throughout the world would have given anything to see . . . Alec Ramsay and the Black racing again!

Preston

18

For more than an hour after leaving Leesburg, the horse van traveled across the dusty hot road of the broad plateau. Reaching the northern range, it began climbing, and soon left the heated air behind. At first the ascent was a gradual one across rounded hills, but within a short while the road became steeper as it wound through the ever rising mountains. With the setting of the sun the road turned gray in the twilight, and finally blackness enveloped the van. Headlights came on to pierce the night, the van was put in low gear, moving slowly, cautiously up the steep grades.

Within the close confines of the van, the boy and stallion were aware of the precipitous climb only because of the slanting floor. The stallion had his long legs spread apart, with the straw rising above his fetlocks. McGregor sat in a canvas chair in front of him, watching him and listening to the steady pull of the engine. Its pitch was low, too low for what he wanted to associate with it. There was also the noise from the slow turning of rubber wheels on well-packed gravel. This wasn't the same, either.

He watched the stallion reach for the hay in the rope-mesh sling in front of his stall. He saw him pull it out and begin chewing. He listened to the sound of his hoofs in the straw when the stallion shifted his weight. He watched him shake his head, pulling taut the cross ropes that held him. The blanket slipped down on his neck.

McGregor got to his feet, and pulled the blanket up again. His hands stayed on the stallion's neck, his touch soft and gentle. He talked to the horse. He watched the ears come forward, the stallion turning and listening. He waited. Any second, any moment that black mental curtain would rise, and he would remember *everything*.

His lips were drawn in a fine thin line as he tried to make his memory return. He felt he could do it now, this moment, if only he made a *great effort* to remember.

The van lurched as it was thrown into still lower gear to ease the strain of the climb. McGregor found himself noticing the steeper pitch of the floor. The stallion snorted with tossing head. McGregor turned to the blanketed body. He read the white letters on the maroon background. "The Allen Ranch."

He closed his eyes. He mustn't look at the blanket or the sloping floor of the van . . . or even his horse. He must shut his ears to the sound of the engine, and where it was taking him. He must concentrate only on what he wanted to know. He must make a great effort. His demand must come from within. He must . . .

But he found he could not close his mind as he had his eyes. It was not that easy. As he thought of Preston and all the people who would be watching him tomorrow, he felt a terrible fear rising within him. He looked at his horse, and found that his terror was mirrored in the stallion's eyes.

There came a snort and the pawing of a muscled foreleg. Thin-skinned nostrils were blown out. The cross ropes became taut as the stallion shook his head.

Realizing that his fear was causing the stallion's restlessness, McGregor turned away from him. He went to the chair and sat down. He told himself that he wanted to race the stallion for Allen, that at times during the past few days he had even looked forward to it. No harm would come to him. He would be back at the ranch by tomorrow night. The terror that now gripped him was due only to their being on their way, leaving behind for a short while the protection, the security he had known at the ranch. He would get used to it. He would be all right by the time they reached Preston.

He remained in the chair until his fear had left him. He made no further effort to bring back his memory. He realized that he couldn't concentrate, couldn't demand to know anything now . . . not with tomorrow's race so near. After the race, when he was back at the ranch, it might be different. But now he could only wait, wait as he had been doing for what already seemed a lifetime.

An hour later, the van reached the crest of the range

and began its descent. It went no faster than it had during the long climb, and at times much slower. The road turned and twisted, dropping abruptly alongside tremendous cliffs. Mile after mile the van descended, wallowing in the blackness of the great walls that rose higher and higher above it to shut out the dim illumination of the stars.

After a long while, the van left the canyon, picking up speed as it went through a valley surrounded on every side by towering rock. The road led to another mountain range many miles away. After an hour the van slowed, and crossed a long bridge. Far below was a tremendous chasm, and deep within its bowels flowed a river. The moon turned the water into a silver ribbon, brilliant yet seemingly unmoving in the great depth of the canyon.

On the other side of the bridge the van picked up speed again. The high peaks ahead were no closer than before, but the van had gained open country now, mounting and descending little flat hills covered with sage. Finally, as it descended one of the hills, the lights of Preston could be seen in the distance.

The van surged forward until it neared the outskirts of the city. The mass of buildings rose feebly in comparison to the towering mountain range beyond, but their lights shone brightly in the night . . . red, green and white, going on and off along street after street.

The van passed the railroad station, and then crossed the tracks. It glided into the city on wheels that turned smoothly, almost noiselessly, on paved streets. It went down broad avenues, slowing to the speed that had taken it up the steepest of the mountain grades, but for a

different reason. The way was filled with people over-
flowing from the sidewalks. Cattlemen, prospectors, min-
ers, sheepherders, and Indians had descended upon
Preston for three days of celebration. Long-legged cowboys and punchers, dressed in skin-tight Levis, colorful
silk shirts, and broad sombreros, were there from near
and far to take home prize money. They would partici-
pate in the bronc-busting, bull-dogging, and calf-tying
contests. They would enter the fastest of their horses in
the races. Indians from the reservations mingled with
them, some squatting on the sidewalks, trying to sell their
pottery, baskets and beadwork; others ignoring the con-
fusion of the crowd, waiting aloof and patiently for
tomorrow's horse racing, a sport they loved and understood above all others. They, too, would race, for as
Navajos they had been taught to ride almost in their
infancy, and horses were their most prized possessions.

The van wound its way through the streets, sometimes
stopping and waiting for the mass of people to give it
room to pass. There were cars and taxis and buses having
no easier time of it. Slowly the van passed the park and
the hotels, the stores and restaurants. Finally it came to
the broad highway leading out of the city. It passed
tourist courts, jammed, like the city behind, with cars
and people. Another mile, and it passed the airport with
the tower beacon turning slowly in the night. A short
distance beyond was the city's race track.

The van turned off the highway, and crossed the plain
to the half-mile oval. Along the track's homestretch were
uncovered bleacher stands, and across the way a line of
open stables. Horses stood beneath bare light bulbs.

Other horses were stabled in trailers, vans, and in tents behind the sheds.

Allen's van passed the stable area, and kept going until it was beyond the turn of the track. There in the darkness it stopped.

McGregor waited for the side door to be opened. He knew they had arrived. He had known it for a long time, from the noise of downtown Preston to the shrill neighs and nickering of horses here at the track.

"Mac?"

"Yes, boss." He could see the dim outline of Allen's head and shoulders when the door was opened.

"You want to walk the kinks out of his legs? Hank thinks it would be best."

"No. We'll stay here. I'm going to turn him loose in the van for the rest of the night. That's all the exercise he'll need."

Allen said nothing. McGregor heard him whispering to Larom, and then, "Where'll *you* sleep, Mac?"

"In the stall, so he won't be stepping on me."

"Okay, but bed down the back of the van, then. I don't want him slipping on the bare floor."

"Yes, boss."

Again McGregor saw their heads come together, and heard their whispered consultation.

Allen said finally, "Hank will be sleeping in the front seat, Mac. Call him if you need him."

"I will, boss. Good night."

"'Night, Mac. You got a light?"

"Yes, boss."

The door closed, and a few moments later McGregor heard Larom climb into the van's cab. Apparently he had been ordered to stick close by until time for the race. Allen was taking no chance of McGregor's not being around in the morning.

Turning on his flashlight, he took several bales of straw, and bedded down the back of the van. Then he hung buckets of water and feed in the far corner, and turned the stallion loose. His horse moved from the stall and walked around the van, sniffing and snorting until he found his feed.

McGregor cleaned the stall, and then unfolded his portable canvas cot. Within a few minutes he was lying on it, and listening to the movements of his horse. He could smell the wood smoke from the fires a short distance away. He knew what it was like down there. He could see the bandages, cloths and coolers hanging on the lines. He was aware of the excitement and anticipation that was sweeping through men and horses alike. He could hear the good-natured calls, the whistling, the humming of men while they cared for their horses. All this was typical of the night before the races. Tomorrow it would be different. Men and horses would awaken to the seriousness of the day. There would be no laughing, no loud shouts in the stable area. They would leave all that to the people in the stands, those who had come only to watch. The backside of the track would know only tenseness, a long period of waiting before being called to the post.

No visitors today. No hay today. We go to the post at one o'clock.

He knew what it was like now, and what it would be like tomorrow. He knew everything except *where* he had learned it all, and *when*. He closed his eyes, not wanting to think about it any more, and asking only for sleep to come. He concentrated on the unceasing movements of his horse as he walked about the van, working the stiffness out of his legs. Finally the constant rustling of hoofs in the deep straw put him to sleep.

He awakened to the gray light of dawn coming through the high window behind him. He saw that the stallion was stretched out down on the straw. He was glad his horse had gotten off his feet during the night. It was a good sign. He moved on his cot, and the stallion's head came up and turned toward him. "This is it," he told him softly. "This is the day."

Hearing someone at the door, he got to his feet. Larom was outside, carrying two pails.

"Morning, Mac. Here's some fresh water."

"Thanks, Hank." McGregor watered his horse and then returned to Larom, saying, "He should get out for a while this morning."

"I know, but Allen doesn't want him on the track. He's got some funny idea about springin' him all at once on everybody, includin' Herbert and Night Wind. I don't get it, but he's the boss."

The boy turned away from the door. He went to the stallion again, and this time gave him some grain. He knew that he was responsible for Allen's not wanting the stallion seen until post time. He had told Allen that it was best to keep him away from other horses, so that he would not become overexcited. He had told him, too, that if knowledge of the stallion's swiftness could be kept from Herbert they would have an advantage in the race.

"Where is Ralph Herbert?" he asked Larom.

"In town, but that ain't makin' any difference," Larom said. "His trainer and boys are over there with Night Wind. We take our horse on the track this morning, and Herbert and the town would know all about him before noon. The boss says to keep him away from them, and that's what we're doing."

"Where's the boss?"

"He caught a ride into town last night, figuring to stay there, and let Herbert know we're all set to go."

"What's to stop Herbert from coming out here and finding us?"

Larom smiled. "Several hundred vans just like ours, and most of 'em carryin' horses. Allen says Herbert ain't the kind of guy to spend all morning just lookin' for a horse." He turned toward the track. "Things are just startin' to stir down there. Can't even get a cup of coffee yet, and we only had one sandwich since we left the ranch."

The boy's gaze was on the broad expanse of endless plain to the west. The sky above it was still dark. "Let me take him out there," he said. "He only needs a light gallop. Allen said to keep him off the track, but he didn't say anything about not working him out there."

"No, he didn't say anything about that." Larom turned his dark, leathery face toward the boy. "But he said I should stick close to you, and I got no horse."

"But why, Hank? What does he think I might do anyway?"

"I don't know why. It ain't my orders. It's his. He's got his own notions. I guess he's just playin' it safe. He don't want anything to happen to you. I can't blame him. He ain't playin' for pennies, not with Hot Feet up as his part of the purse he ain't. And if you don't ride that black horse no one else is goin' to do it."

"But you want us to win, don't you?"

"I ain't sayin' nothin' but that."

"Then you'd better let me gallop him," McGregor said quietly. "He's had more than five hours of hard traveling and six more hours of just waiting around here. Give him a chance to stretch out now, and he'll come back all ready to race."

For a moment Larom was undecided, and then he said, "Okay, Mac. I guess it'll be all right. No one will see you out there."

A little later McGregor led the saddled stallion down the ramp. Larom boosted him up, and said, "You work him like you think you should, but don't go far, Mac."

The boy's hand was on the black neck. "Quit worrying, Hank. This will only take a few minutes." He let the stallion go.

They left the ever lightening sky of early morning behind them. He kept the stallion at a mild gallop, wanting him only to loosen up. He felt the great hoofs come down upon the ground without a jar. He leaned forward, whispering softly into ears that flicked back at the sound of his voice. He knew the stallion wanted to run all out. He told him that it was not time, that they must wait a few more hours. Now they were just to gallop easily and without strain. The rest would come later.

He took him a half-mile, and then turned, coming back at a slow lope. Standing in his stirrups, he did not look at Hank Larom, who was impatiently awaiting their return. Instead he looked beyond the man, toward the land beneath the distant, dull-gray sky. Out there and not so many miles away was the beginning of the deep canyon country. No one, not even Allen, who was so afraid that something might happen to him, realized that only yester-day he had fleetingly considered riding the great stallion into that country where no one would ever find them.

He spurned the thought now as he had then. He turned away from its beckoning, knowing that he did not have to run again, that soon he would be back at the ranch.

Later, after he had cooled out the stallion and left him blanketed in the big van, he went to the stable area with Larom. They found the kitchen tent with its long counter and stools, and sat down.

The early morning air was brisk, but that was not the reason McGregor pulled up his jacket collar high on his neck. He was afraid of being recognized. But his fear left him almost immediately. There were too many men shouting and clamoring for anyone to pay much attention to him. He had no special identity in this carefree throng of swaggering cowboys. He tried to be one of them; it was the easiest way to avoid suspicion.

While he sat on the stool, awaiting his breakfast, he wondered why the stable area wasn't the same as he had expected. These men were gay and laughing. They were enjoying themselves. Where was the tenseness, that long period of dreadful waiting before being called to the post? Where were the grim faces and the silent men who walked up and down before their barns until even in the coolness of early morning their shirts would be wet with sweat? Not here certainly. Yet he had expected it to be this way. Why? Because it had been that way for him *before*? Yes, that was his answer.

After breakfast they returned to the van, and found Allen awaiting them. They all climbed into the back of the van, and sat there quietly, watching the black stallion. The boy turned to Allen many times. Here was more what he had known before. Here was a grim face, a tortured face, that knew the pain of waiting. He turned to Larom, and found that his face disclosed everything that was in Allen's. He found himself wondering about his own face. Was the agony of waiting written there, too?

He said, "Just a couple more hours now." He hardly recognized his own voice, and he realized then that he looked and felt no different from the two men.

An hour before the race they convinced themselves that they should get a cup of coffee. They went to the kitchen tent again. They spoke only to give their orders. McGregor sat between them, and waited for his coffee, waited for the race to begin. It wouldn't be long now. Post time for the match race was one o'clock. It was to be the first race on the day's program. Across the track the stands had filled with spectators long ago. Hundreds more were already standing around the half-mile oval, and there was an endless stream of cars still coming from the highway.

"I wish this thing was over."

The voice came from McGregor's right, and he thought Allen had spoken. But it wasn't Allen, for his employer had turned to the man sitting beside him. He was a small man, different from all others here because he wore no wide-rimmed sombrero, and no colorful silk shirt. His face was pinched and wizened, as was the rest of him except for his hands. They were giant-size.

McGregor turned away quickly, pulling his sombrero down close to his eyes. He had known this man before. He knew this, but nothing else . . . not where or when, only that the slight figure had stepped from behind the black mental barrier of lost time.

The man was talking to Allen. "I ride Night Wind," he said. "I'm a contract rider for High Crest Ranch. I got no beef. Herbert tells me to ride and I ride. But what he makes me come here for, I don't know. I miss a couple of good rides at Santa Anita today because he calls me, and says get to Preston! Sure I come. If I don't, I break my contract, and I'm fired. I don't get to ride Night Wind at Santa Anita or nowhere else. I ain't dumb enough to let a thing like that get by me. But why he gets me to ride in this jerk rodeo circus, I don't know. Night Wind don't need me up on him to win here. As I say, I got no beef with Herbert. He's paying me all right, and I get his best horses to ride. But why he didn't get one of his ranch boys to ride this race, I don't know. Why he gets me to come all the way from California for this thing, I don't know."

Allen finished his coffee, and turned on his stool. "I

don't know either," he said, getting to his feet. Only when they were leaving the tent did he speak again. "I didn't expect Herbert to get his top rider here. Herbert is out for blood, all right." His face was white.

"Hot Feet, y'mean," Larom said.

McGregor said nothing.

They pushed their way through the packed crowd in the stable area, having to look at the laughing faces, having to listen to the gay, carnival spirit that had swept over the grounds. They walked single file, following each other with McGregor in the lead, for it was he who wanted most to get away. Suddenly he stopped, his eyes on the tall man coming toward him. Fear choked him. He wanted to turn and run, but could only stand still. He knew the man and he didn't have to ask himself when he had last seen him. The heavy-set frame, the round face, the gray suit, and gray sombrero, the bright silver star . . . *the sheriff from Leesburg!* Close behind him was another man McGregor recognized . . . *Cruikshank,* with his gaunt body stooped, the more easily to move through the crowd.

Somehow he knew they had come for him! He turned on leaden feet and tried to run. He bumped into Allen. His employer's face showed surprise and then alarm when McGregor tried to break away from him. A hand from behind fell on the boy's shoulder, and he heard the sheriff say, "You're wanted on suspicion of robbery and murder, kid."

The Sprung Trap

19

"Murder!" McGregor mouthed the word, but it never left his bloodless lips. He looked at Allen. He saw the rancher's face lengthen until the skin was drawn tight and white. He watched him try to smile, a thin, sickly opening of the mouth.

"You're joking, Tom," Allen said. "It's no time for stuff like that. We're going to race in just a few minutes."

McGregor heard the sheriff's reply, while the heavy hand remained on his shoulder, the fingers deep in his flesh. "No, Irv. I'm not kidding." There was sympathy in the sheriff's voice, but resoluteness as well. "The whole state's been alerted to be on the lookout for him. He's wanted in Utah . . . a diner stick-up . . . The three men who worked with him on the job have been caught." His voice dropped a little. "The diner's cashier died a

227

couple of weeks ago from injuries they gave him at the time.''

Allen turned to the boy. "Let's get out of here, Tom," he said. "We can't talk here."

"There's only one place for me to take him," the sheriff said quietly.

"I want to know more before you do that." Allen's eyes had left the boy, and there was fury in his gaze when he looked at the haggard face of the man standing the sheriff. "I want to know what Cruikshank had to do with this."

The sheriff shifted his big frame uneasily, but his eyes and voice were steady when he said, "Cruikshank just tipped me off, Irv. He pointed out to me what I hadn't noticed at all . . . that the description of the kid wanted in Salt Lake City fits McGregor." The sheriff paused before adding, "If you want to get out of here and hear the rest, I guess it'll be all right."

McGregor was pulled around, and then directed through the crowd. He didn't raise his eyes. He didn't care any longer. He was wanted for *murder*. There would be no more running.

They stopped before the van; there were no people this far from the track. He heard one of the stallion's hoofs strike wood, and then it was quiet inside again. Maybe they'd let him see him once more. Maybe, if Allen asked the sheriff, he'd be allowed inside the van for the last time.

The sheriff said, "Here's the state circular I've had hanging in my office, Irv, and attached to it is the news clipping Cruikshank gave me last night, when he reminded me of the kid who was working for you.''

Allen read the details of the robbery, and the description of the missing boy. He turned to study McGregor.

The sheriff said, "You see the description fits, don't you, Irv?"

"Yes, but you're not certain it's he," Allen said. "You're taking him to jail only on suspicion."

The sheriff tried to smile. "That's all they sent me on him, Irv. If the description fits, I got to take him in." He turned to McGregor. "And the kid isn't denying anything. You even saw him try to get away back there, when he saw me coming."

Allen turned to the boy. "Mac," he said, "did you do it? Are you the one they want?" He couldn't get McGregor to raise his eyes from the ground. "You can tell me, Mac," he went on softly. "I'll help you all I can, *if* you did do it. We'll fight it. Remember, Mac, if it's you they want, you were only the lookout for those men, *grown men*. You're nothing but a kid. They could have forced you to go with them."

They waited for him to lift his gaze, to say something. But he did neither. He couldn't. What good would it do to tell them he didn't know? It wouldn't help. And he *did* remember certain gruesome details . . . the great swelling on the crown of his head, the terrible pain that had stayed with him for days afterward, the raw and bleeding hands, the dark-stained money he had found in his pocket. Yet Allen was trying to convince him that he might not have had anything to do with fatally injuring the cashier. Where, then, could he have received his own injuries except in a fight?

The wafting call of a bugle rose above the distant wave of voices. When it ended, and its lingering note had died down, there came a great roar of acclamation. Even McGregor raised his head and turned his eyes in the direction of the horse moving before the stands. *Night Wind had answered the call to the post.*

Allen's face was white. Finally he said, "Hank, you'd better tell them the race is off."

Larom didn't leave. Instead he turned to the sheriff as the roar of the crowd rang in their ears. The sheriff dropped his gaze and said, "We'd better get going, kid. Don't give me any trouble now."

Larom said quietly, "It doesn't take very long for a horse to run a mile, Tom."

The sheriff knew what Larom was asking, and he shook his head. Allen knew, too, but he only said, "I'll go along with you, Mac. Hank can stay here."

"I'm sorry, Irv," the sheriff said. "I know what this race meant to you."

"It's harder to lose before a race than after," Allen said. His voice shook, and he knew he fooled no one. "The kid's in a jam. I want to help him, if I can. There'll be other races."

"But no other horses for you like Hot Feet," the sheriff reminded him.

Swift, disturbed anger came to Allen's face. "Quit it, Tom," he said bitterly. "You got what you came for, so let's go."

The sheriff still didn't move. Suddenly Cruikshank said, "Ain't goin' to stay here for the whole day, are we, sheriff? Take'm, an' pen him up like ya' done t'me."

They all turned to him, and Larom said, "You timed it good, Cruikshank. You couldn't have timed it better."

"Don't know what ya' mean, Hank. I seen my duty an' I done it." Cruikshank's pitted black eyes were bright and shifting. "Let's get him in, sheriff."

The sheriff shifted his weight against Cruikshank's prodding shoulder. "We'll go when I say to go, and not before," he said.

The sound of the bugle came again. The crowd was no longer shouting, only impatient for the race to begin. The stands shook to the rhythmical stomping of feet.

Allen said, "Hank, I told you to go and tell them it's off."

But Larom didn't leave. Again he caught and held the sheriff's uneasy, *undecided* eyes. "Tom," he said with quiet assurance, "like I just told you, it would be only a few minutes from the time he leaves here and the time he gets back. It would mean a lot to us, and somethin' to the kid, too. He's worked hard on this horse."

"No y'don't!" Cruikshank screamed, and his long fingers tore at McGregor's arm in an attempt to pull him away from the sheriff. "Y'git him in now jus' like you done t'me."

McGregor felt the sheriff's hand again, grabbing and holding him steady against Cruikshank's crazed attempts to yank him away.

"Take your hands off him," the sheriff said in a cutting

voice. Cruikshank's black eyes shifted from the sheriff to the boy, and then back again. Finally he took his hands away.

The sheriff said, "That's better. Now, Hank, you go and tell them that your horse will be coming down in a minute. Irv, I'm letting McGregor ride, but holding you responsible for him until the race is over."

They pushed McGregor toward the van, and opened the door. He saw his horse, and only then did he realize it wasn't the end at all. *With the great stallion he could get away.*

They put the ramp down, and Allen said softly, "Get the horse, Mac. After the race I'll go with you. You needn't be afraid. I'll get the best lawyer. I'll . . ."

But the boy didn't listen. He went into the van, and put on the stallion's bridle and saddle. Then he took him down the ramp. Only the sheriff and Allen were waiting for them . . . these two and the crowd beyond. Cruikshank had gone, beaten again and running . . . just as he, too, would be running within a few minutes. He felt sorry for Cruikshank. He knew what it was like to be beaten, to live with fear, and to hide and run.

Allen boosted him up. "No time to put on silks," he said. "It makes no difference, anyway."

No, racing silks made no difference. McGregor picked up the reins, and felt the stallion surge at his touch. He held him still. The horse was alive with fire today and ready for the race of his life! But not with Night Wind. There wasn't going to be any match race. Instead he and his stallion would be racing toward the deep canyon country, and once there he would stay forever. If it meant death for him, well, he preferred such a death to what the sheriff offered in its place. He didn't plan to let his horse die with him. He'd turn him loose, make him go away, once they were in the great canyons. The stallion would find his way out.

"Ready, kid?" Allen was standing close, his hands hot and shaking on McGregor's leg in the drawn-up stirrup.

The boy nodded, and took his eyes off Allen. He didn't want to look at him, knowing what he was about to do to him. The sheriff was on the other side, and far enough away. Now, if Allen would just step back a few feet, he wouldn't hurt him when he whirled the stallion. He didn't want to hurt anyone. He just wanted to get away. Allen removed his hand from McGregor's leg. *Now,* the boy thought, *now!*

Match Race

20

But Allen didn't step away from the black stallion. Instead he reached for the bridle. He'd never before taken hold of the stallion, but in his great excitement he didn't think of this now. For the moment he'd forgotten all caution. He was thinking only of the race to come, the race that a few minutes ago had been hopelessly lost to him. Now he was taking *his entry* to the post. The crowd was waiting for them. After the race he'd do all he could for McGregor. But he needn't think of that now. He turned to the sheriff. "Tom," he said, "you'll find a racing whip in the tack trunk. Please get it for me." He began walking.

The boy hardly breathed, his head reeled, when his horse stepped forward obediently beneath Allen's hand. This wasn't as he'd planned. The stallion was eager to go along with Allen. McGregor sat back in the saddle, his spine stiff. He could do nothing but await an opportunity to be free of Allen. He rose in his stirrups and leaned forward again, talking to the stallion, reminding him that he was there. But the small head never tossed or turned in understanding of his sounds and touches. There was no flicking back of pricked ears to listen to him. The stallion's senses were keyed to what lay ahead.

Allen kept walking, taking them ever closer to the track. The boy saw the faces of the crowd beginning to turn in their direction, and he knew he had to get away at once, regardless of what happened to Allen. He drew back on the reins. Allen turned to him quickly, his gaze startled and searching. McGregor was ready to pull his horse around when the sheriff's towering figure came up beside them. Again McGregor had to wait. He watched the sheriff pass the whip to Allen.

Suddenly the short leather whip was in his own hand, and Allen was leading the stallion again. McGregor didn't remember relinquishing his tight hold of the reins. He was looking at the whip, his nails pressed deep into its leather. He was aware of nothing but the feel of it in his hand. He didn't want the whip, yet he couldn't drop it. He stared at it. Why did he know he should never touch the stallion with it? *Why?*

They were on the track. The stands were a sea of swarming, indistinct faces, strangely quiet while the stallion moved in front of them. Then came a mounting hum of excited voices until suddenly the air was shattered by a continuous roar.

Allen smiled, knowing the crowd was for him and his entry. Night Wind was a Texas thoroughbred, an outsider, while he and his horse *belonged*.

The track announcer said over the public address system, "Coming on the track is Range Boss, owned by the Allen Ranch of Leesburg, Arizona."

The boy felt his blood run hot while the shouts of the crowd rang in his ears. The stallion sidestepped across the track, pulling Allen into a run. McGregor heard himself say to Allen, "Better let go of him now. I'll take him up."

Allen turned the stallion loose, but he remained on the track, sharing his entry's glory. His eyes stayed on the stallion, but his ears were tuned to the voices from the stands, taking in the great acclamation while the black horse moved past. Allen loved every moment of it. Last year it had been this way with Hot Feet. But that had been *after* the race, he reminded himself, when Hot Feet had won the three-year-old crown. This was much too early to feel as he did. His face sobered, and he hurried to catch up to the black stallion.

Going past the stands, the boy held a tight rein. He tried to close his ears to the *familiar*, clamoring cries. He wanted to listen only to the lone beat of hoofs that told him he was free of Allen. Nothing could keep him from leaving now. All he had to do was to take the stallion to the far side of the track and go over the low fence. He'd be on his way before the sheriff or Allen realized what he was doing.

"Go now," he told himself savagely. *"What are you waiting for?"*

The whip was clenched in his hand. He felt his flesh crawl at the touch of it. How long had he been staring at the whip? He turned his eyes away. The stallion snorted and moved faster, hating the tight rein that held him to a slow walk. McGregor rose higher in his stirrups, looking over the small head. He saw the starting gate, stretched halfway across the track. The wire-mesh doors in front were closed. To the right of the gate was a high platform, and standing there was the official starter.

"Hurry that horse!" The starter tried to keep the impatience out of his voice.

All this was so familiar, to McGregor and to the stallion. Couldn't Allen and all the others see that this was no outlaw horse he rode, that he and the stallion had gone to the post before? Even so, what did it matter *now*?

He'd had no intention of going so far, but now he found himself taking his horse around the gate. He felt the mounting tension within him. The stallion shook his head savagely, trying to get more rein. McGregor kept him near the rail and away from the horse who stood just in back of the gate. He turned the stallion's head toward the far turn, yet his own eyes remained on the dark brown horse with white markings on face and legs. He had seen Night Wind before. He was certain of this, too.

He let the stallion lengthen out going away from the gate. He felt reassured of his means of escape in those swift, easy strides. Finally he rose high in his stirrups, and brought the stallion down to a prancing walk. Then he turned him around. He was going back to the gate, even going inside to come out on the break. All the way down the track, he asked himself, *"Why?"* His only answer was that it didn't matter how they reached the backstretch just as long as they got there. One way around the oval was as good as another. Yet he knew he was lying, that something over which he had no control was taking him and his horse to the starting gate.

The stallion's eyes were on Night Wind. He screamed once and his loud challenge silenced the stands. For a moment every gaze was on him. He came close to the gate, his great black body glistening in the sun, and there was a savage wildness to his action.

One of the starter's assistants walked toward him, and the man's movement broke the stillness of the stands. There came the drone of excited whisperings, for the spectators had caught a glimpse of what they had been told to expect, yet hadn't believed. The Allen Ranch was racing a stallion that had run wild only two weeks ago!

McGregor watched the assistant starter come toward them. He saw the fright in the man's eyes when he reached for the bridle. The stallion reared.

"Get back," McGregor said, bringing his horse down. "I'll take him in alone."

As he moved away, the man said, "Hurry him up then. You got a whip. Use it on him, if you have to!"

Use it on him, if you have to!

The words seemed to tear McGregor's ears apart. He raised the whip before his eyes, staring at it for many seconds. He felt the tears come suddenly, burning his eyelids. Why was he crying? The tears came faster, blinding him. He brushed his hand over them, angrily sweeping them away. He looked toward the stands, searching for the person who had called those very same words to him an eternity ago. The sea of faces swarmed before him. He looked harder, finding Allen, and Larom, and the sheriff on the rail . . . the only faces he knew. He saw a figure suddenly appear behind them, and for a flickering second hope rose within him. Then he recognized Gordon, and turned his attention back to the gate.

At his command, the stallion moved quickly into his starting stall, and the gate closed behind them. There was only one way out now. When the door in front opened there'd be no turning back, *ever*.

He didn't look at the horse and rider in the next stall. His eyes were focused straight ahead and he was looking through the wire mesh at the track that lay before him, so golden in the sun. Suddenly he gasped. And as the air rushed out of his lungs, he knew that here was the true road back that had evaded him for so long, the road that would have told him everything he wanted to know, if he'd found it yesterday or any of the long days before it. Now it wasn't important. Now it was just a means of escape!

The track announcer said, "The horses are at the post." The spectators were quiet, awaiting the start. Their eyes were on the front door of the gate. They didn't want to miss a thing. They knew that a world of horsepower was ready to explode in a single race. This was to be no usual sprint of three hundred or four hundred yards, but a long mile, twice around the track. This was to be a very special race, and they awaited it in hushed silence.

At the rail near the starting gate, Ralph Herbert removed his horn-rimmed glasses, and quickly wiped the sweat from his eyes. "I don't like this," he told his trainer, a man with a frame as solid and big as his own. "Allen has put something over on us. That black horse isn't fresh off the range. Did you see how he walked into his stall?"

"Yeah, I saw." The trainer worked his jutting square jaw. "But he's wild enough to fight at the drop of a rein. If anything should happen to Night Wind . . ."

"Nothing will happen to him," Herbert said. "But that kid sure can handle that black horse. Look how he's quieting him down, after all his twisting."

"Who is the kid, anyway?"

"Allen said his name's McGregor. Works at the ranch."

"He looks familiar to me," the trainer said, "as I mentioned before."

"Yeah, I know. I'd like to see him without that hat. He's got it pulled far enough down to pretty near cover his eyes."

"And that horse is like something we've seen before, too. He's no mustang, that's for sure. He's bigger than Night Wind and hot-blooded, Ralph."

Herbert said, "I know it. I'm worried. Allen's sprung a race horse on us."

"Maybe so. But there's no doubt that horse has run wild, and done a lot of fighting, Ralph. He's been cut up plenty. Look at his scars."

"I'm still worried."

The trainer smiled. "What for, Ralph? So he's a race

horse, and that's why Allen agreed so readily to the mile distance. You think anything here is going to beat Night Wind? Our horse is better than he was last year. You know that as well as I do. If you're going to worry, save it for Santa Anita, when we'll be up against the best again. Even then I won't be worrying, not if Night Wind keeps running the way he's been going."

Herbert nodded. "I suppose you're right. But just the same I'm glad I have Eddie Malone up on him. I've got ten of my best quarter mares at stake in this race."

"I know that, all right," his trainer answered. "Just don't worry, Ralph."

A short distance down the rail Allen felt a hand from behind grab his arm. He didn't turn. He couldn't take his eyes from the horses in the gate. Any second they'd be off. But Larom and the sheriff turned to the man behind, and Larom said, "Hello, Slim. I didn't think anything would get you this far from Leesburg!"

Allen felt Gordon's fingers digging deeper into his arm, and then Gordon said, "That kid is *Alec Ramsay* and the horse is the *Black*. Alec Ramsay and the Black! Did you hear what I said, Allen?" His voice was shrill.

Without turning to him, Allen asked, "You mean McGregor?"

"McGregor nothing. That's not his name. *It's Alec Ramsay!*"

Allen shrugged his shoulders. The kid had the stallion quiet. The break was coming. "What's the difference what his name is, Slim? He's wanted by the police in Salt Lake City. Tom's here to pick him up."

"You're all crazy!" Gordon shouted. "He hasn't done

anything! He's Alec Ramsay and the horse is the Black. They're famous, I tell you! Their plane crashed in Wyoming and . . ." The roar of the crowd droned out his words.

"THEY'RE OFF!"

With the opening of the doors, the stallion broke from the boy's restraining hands, and came out of the gate in front of Night Wind. McGregor caught a glimpse of the white blaze at his horse's flanks, and then it fell behind quickly as the black stallion's strides steadied and began to lengthen. He drew back on the reins. He called to his horse. He didn't want him running all out. Their race wasn't here, but across the plain! The stretch was short. They'd be at the first turn before he'd be able to pull down the stallion.

Allen's eyes were moist as he pounded Larom on the back. "He'll hold that lead! He's got the race, Hank!" His foreman nodded his head vigorously in complete agreement.

Among the thousands who watched, only Herbert and his trainer were silent. They were unimpressed by flying starts from the gate. They knew their champion was built to go a distance, and that his speed would mount steadily until he'd run over anything before him. This was a mile race, and what happened in the first few hundred yards was for fanciers of the quarter horse, and not the thoroughbred. Herbert's clenched hand began pounding the rail, for even now with the horses approaching the first turn Night Wind was gaining!

McGregor slowed the stallion's strides still more. He

drew back on the reins, and kept talking to his horse. He heard the fading roar of the crowd as his mount swept into the turn. The stallion's resentment at the tight rein was felt by McGregor in the terrible pull on his arms. The stallion wanted to run, and was telling him so forcefully.

"Soon," he called, *"but not now!"*

He saw the straining, nut-brown body of Night Wind come up on the outside. His jockey was sitting still in the saddle, not asking Night Wind for more speed, but getting it. Their eyes met for a second. The black stallion lowered his head, pulled harder, and picked up speed. The horses reached the middle of the turn, racing stride for stride, stirrup to stirrup.

The boy's head throbbed. He knew Night Wind wasn't going to be taken to the front because that horse couldn't, *wouldn't* run up there. Once in front Night Wind would relax and start looking around him, forgetting completely about the business at hand unless reminded by his rider.

How did he know this? Why was he so sure of it? *Because he remembered seeing Night Wind do just that in the Belmont Stakes.* Night Wind had gone into the lead at the half-mile pole. He had stopped then to glance at the far stands. He had been whipped by his jockey, and brought on again in the last quarter to win over Hyperion by a head!

McGregor's teeth tore his lips. His memory was coming back! They were entering the backstretch. Here was where they would leave the track. Here was where *his* race would actually begin! He shortened the reins, and the stallion's head came down again. He pulled harder, knowing he would have to fight the stallion to get him off the track.

He saw the look of surprise come to the other rider's face as he succeeded in shortening the stallion's strides, and Night Wind surged ahead. He saw the horse's powerful quarters rise and fall in front of him. He was still watching when Night Wind suddenly relaxed and began to bounce along easily and without effort. Then Night Wind turned his head to the side, interested in the crowd across the infield. His jockey went for the whip, bringing it down solidly on Night Wind's haunches. Once more the whip rose and fell before Night Wind's attention returned to the track ahead, and his strides picked up again.

The boy tried to get the stallion away from the rail and off the track. His fury mounted when the stallion fought him, straining his arms until he could no longer stand the pull. He remembered the whip in his boot and reached for it. Just as he raised it, ready to bring it down, he remembered something else.

A man . . . a short, stocky man standing beside him in the night and wearing only pajamas, his face as white as his disheveled hair . . . a pitchfork in one hand, a whip in the other . . . a raging face and voice saying, "Take the whip. Use it on him if you have to!"

And his own reply in the night, *"If I did, he'd kill me. The same as he would have killed you."*

The whip fell to the track as though he had held a hot coal. His hand seemed to burn, and he placed it on the wet neck before him. Then he leaned forward until his cheek, too, was pressed against his horse. He began talking, sobbing to him. Without realizing what he was doing, he let his hands come up, giving the stallion more rein. He never heard the increased pounding of the lightning hoofs nor was he aware that the backstretch rail was slipping by faster and faster. He was conscious only of the turbulent working of his mind.

The stallion's body and strides were extended until he seemed barely to touch the track. He swept into the back turn, gaining rapidly on the running horse in front of him. Night Wind's jockey glanced back and began using his whip again. But the black stallion's rush was not to be denied. His head was parallel with Night Wind's stirrups as the horses came off the turn and entered the stretch. The crowd was on its feet. Voices shattered the heavens. With still a lap to go, the two horses were racing as one!

Night Wind's jockey rocked in his saddle, using his hands and feet. But he never touched his horse with the whip again, for no longer was it necessary. Night Wind was being challenged, and this was all the champion thoroughbred needed to urge him on to greater speed.

Herbert's fist banged the rail when the horses flashed by him. The kid riding the stallion was making no move. He was sitting absolutely still, almost lifeless, in the saddle, and yet his horse was matching Night Wind stride for stride.

Herbert's trainer said, "Ralph, we got him, I tell you! No horse in the country could get past Night Wind now!"

But the trainer's words provided no solace for Herbert. He had been tricked by Allen. This black horse had raced before. Where had he seen him? Night Wind should have been pulling away from him by now. But he wasn't at all! He was only holding his own.

Not far down the rail, Gordon was screaming at the top of his voice, *"Go, Alec! Go!"* He pushed between Allen and the sheriff to watch the horses pound into the first turn again.

The sheriff shoved back, and said, "Take it easy, Slim. This is just a horse race."

"Just a horse race *nothing*!" Gordon shouted hysterically. "That's Alec Ramsay riding the Black against the fastest thoroughbred in the country! It's the race of the year, and you don't even realize it!"

Allen paid no attention to them. His glazed eyes were on the horses, but they were an indistinct blur to him. "Can anyone see what's happening?" he asked. "Did he get past Night Wind yet?"

"No," Larom answered. "Mac's got a tight hold on him again. He took up rein just after they passed us. That black horse doesn't like it any more than he did before. He's fighting him."

"Why doesn't he let him go?" Allen shouted.

"He's riding. You ask *him*," Larom said.

McGregor shortened the reins still more, despite the stallion's fury. He pulled him down until Night Wind surged a length ahead and then two lengths more as they came off the turn, entering the backstretch. The boy's mind still erupted with fiery currents that afforded him no peace and produced nothing but a great, flowing mass of conflicting and incoherent elements. Yet sometime within the last few seconds had sprung once more the determination that their race was not to take place here on the track but across the plain. Instinctively he had drawn up on the stallion, trying to force him to respond to his will.

He got his horse away from the rail and to the center of the track, paying no attention to the scarlet-clad jockey on Night Wind, who was drawing farther and farther away from them. His eyes were only for the fighting black head that sought to break his tight hold. He got his horse over closer to the outer rail, working the bit against the corners of the stallion's mouth. His horse fought him more furiously than ever before, and then suddenly bolted back to the center of the track. The boy lost his balance and was thrown forward, his hands grasping the stallion's neck. He felt the great body extend itself again in a determined effort to catch Night Wind. He closed his eyes, sobbing. And then the words came tumbling, bubbling from his mouth, *"Black . . . Black . . . Black . . ."*

The reins dropped from his hand, his eyes opened, the words kept coming. *"Black, I'm Alec Ramsay. I remember. My name is Alec Ramsay. It's come. I know. I know!"* Nothing could equal the joy that came to him then. He was free of the darkness. He could remember everything, including his fall from the plane into the treetops, his crashing and tearing through the branches. The details of what had happened after he'd regained consciousness were hazy. But he could remember the groping in the night, the bright headlights, a long ride that had never seemed to end, and then, finally, the desert. Vague though those first hours were to him, he knew that they led directly to Gordon's cottage in the pines, and that he had never been inside a diner, had never taken part in robbery and murder.

All this came to Alec Ramsay in flashing, successive pictures, and then he looked ahead. They were going into the last turn, with Night Wind's lead already reduced to only two lengths! His jockey was swinging his whip back and forth, keeping Night Wind going now that he was running in front all by himself again.

Alec picked up the loose reins. *"Go, Black. Go!"* he called. Now he was one with his horse. He knew it, and so did the Black! The stallion responded to his call with a new and electrifying burst of speed that sent the earth flying from beneath his hoofs. Gone were the uncertainty and the conflicting wills that had kept them apart for most of the race. No longer did the stallion feel the hard, frenzied pull on his mouth that he had never known before this day. Now he heard the familiar ring of a name that made everything all right again.

"Go, Black. Go!"

Every muscle of the great stallion was strained to its utmost. He came off the turn, drawing alongside the dark-brown champion in great, sweeping strides.

The roar of the crowd split Alec's ears, and now it was no different for him here at Preston than it had been at Belmont Park or Churchill Downs. They were in the stretch drive. He strained with his horse, lifting and urging. He hardly breathed. His hat flew off. Night

Wind's jockey was riding as if his very life depended upon it. For a few seconds the brown horse matched strides with the Black, and then Night Wind began to fall rapidly behind. His rider turned to Alec, and sudden recognition came to his eyes when he saw the boy without his hat.

Alec let out a yell. There was nothing more to this race! He remembered all the classic victories he had seen Night Wind win last year, and yet the Black, *who hadn't raced in years,* was running him into the ground! The stallion's strides became ever greater as he swept gloriously down the homestretch. His hoofs pounded with a thunderous rhythm that silenced the voices in the stands. He was a black flame. He was not a horse but a phantom, a flying black shadow in the eyes of the spectators. And they watched him finish the race in quiet homage.

The stands didn't come to life until long after he had left the homestretch. Even then there was no thunderous ovation, only the cries of people asking if what they had witnessed had been seen by others. There were just nods in reply, and none of the spectators took their eyes off the other side of the track where the giant black horse had been brought to a stop. Finally he was turned around and brought back toward them.

Conclusion

21

Ralph Herbert moved dazedly among the people standing at the rail until he had reached Allen. His face was white, and for a moment he had to struggle to make the words come. He *knew.* He had known all during that last drive, when he had seen the black stallion running so low and pointed, so magnificent in the strides that had taken him far ahead of Night Wind. In flashing seconds, he had remembered another time in Chicago, when he had seen the Black race. And as they came down the stretch, he had identified the Black's rider.

Finally he was able to get the words out. *"Allen, that was Alec Ramsay and the Black!"*

Allen was thinking of the ten mares he would get from High Crest Ranch, and what he would do with them. "I don't care what names you and Slim Gordon give those two," he said. "They're Range Boss and McGregor to me.'' He paused, studying Herbert's shocked face. ''We won, Ralph. You're not trying to get out of your end of the purse, are you?''

"But the Black! He and Alec Ramsay are supposed to be . . ."

''I tell you that horse is what I said he was,'' Allen interrupted angrily. He was beginning to get worried. ''Ask Hank. Ask anyone who was with us. We caught him on the upper range. Right, Hank?''

''Right, boss.'' Larom turned to Herbert. ''We still got his band of mares back at the ranch. And if you need more convincing, take a look at those scars on him when he comes up. He didn't get those in any corral.''

''But . . . but I . . . I'm certain,'' Herbert stammered.

''I'm certain too, Ralph.''

The sheriff said, ''Let's go, Irv. I've got to take him in now.''

Gordon reached for Allen when the rancher bent to get beneath the rail. ''Herbert's right. You've no idea what you're in for.''

Allen came up on the track side. ''Sure I do, Slim. Mac's being booked by the sheriff on suspicion of robbery, and I'm on my way to help him.'' He followed the sheriff down the track.

Herbert asked incredulously, ''Do they think they're taking him to jail?''

Gordon nodded.

''Don't they know what's been going on? Haven't they heard of the *Black* and *Alec Ramsay*?''

''There's your answer,'' Gordon said, nodding toward

the three men walking down the track. "They don't have much use for news outside of what goes on in Leesburg."

"They'll learn soon enough."

"Just as soon as I can get to a phone," Gordon said. He moved quickly through the crowd.

Alec rode the Black into the stretch, hardly conscious of the wild uproar from the stands. He kept repeating his name, just to hear it again. He wanted to get to a telephone right away. He wanted to call *home.* More than two months had passed since the accident. What did his parents and Henry think had happened to him? What had happened to the plane? To the pilot and the copilot? The plane must have crashed. How else would the Black have gotten free? He rubbed his horse's neck. And what was the Black doing here, so many hundreds of miles from Wyoming? Was it a fantastic coincidence that they were together? Or had the stallion's wild, uncanny instinct brought him here? Alec knew all his questions except the last would be answered as soon as he could get to a phone.

Allen approached him. "Mac, what a race!"

Alec tried to keep his voice steady. "Boss," he said, "my name isn't McGregor. It's Ramsay, Alec Ramsay."

Allen turned to the sheriff, and then back to the boy again. "I know," he said kindly. "We've heard that."

No longer did Alec make any attempt to conceal his excitement. *"Who* could have told you, boss? I didn't know myself until a couple of minutes ago."

Allen was puzzled. "Y'mean you didn't know your own name?"

"I'd been hurt. I lost my memory. I haven't been able

to remember a thing about myself—who I was, why I was here, anything at all.''

"Oh,'' Allen said, and then he smiled as he turned to the sheriff. "Tom, you heard what he said. He's been sick a long time, *mentally* sick. He didn't know what he was doing. A good lawyer ought to make a real good case out of something like that, shouldn't he?''

"I sure would think so, Irv. If he had amnesia like he says, he couldn't be held responsible for his actions. Providing, of course,'' he added hastily, "he was in that mental state at the time of the robbery.''

Alec's face had frozen. He looked at the sheriff, remembering suddenly why he was there. "But I didn't . . .'' He stopped, knowing that whatever he said now wouldn't convince them that he'd had no part in the Salt Lake City robbery. Besides, it didn't matter. All this could be straightened out later. "Can I use the phone when we get to wherever it is you're taking me?'' he asked.

"Of course you can,'' the sheriff said. "As Irv says, we're going to do all we can to help you, Mac.''

Alec rode the Black toward the track gate. A bugle sounded, calling the horses in the next race to the post. The Black tossed his head, and sidestepped with marvelous ease and swiftness. He seemed eager to race again.

Allen said, "We'll put Range Boss in the van, and leave Hank here to watch him, Mac. You and I will go into town with Tom. Don't you worry none. Everything's goin' to turn out all right.''

Alec nodded. To Allen he always would be McGregor and the Black would be Range Boss. It would have been funny under any other circumstances.

An hour later Alec Ramsay sat in the Preston court-house. His fingerprints had been taken and sent to the Salt Lake City police. He had been booked on suspicion of robbery and murder. Finally he was given permission by the Preston police captain to use the telephone.

His voice trembled while he placed the long-distance call. Now the phone was ringing at home. His heart pumped harder.

"Hello." His mother had answered.

"Mom. Mom! It's me!" There was silence at the other end. "Mom, can you hear me? It's Alec!" Now came only terrible, wracking sobs from his mother, and he suddenly realized the shock his call must be to her. "Mom. Mom. Don't try to talk. Just listen. I'm alive, and in Preston, Arizona. Preston, Arizona. Can you hear me, Mom?"

The wire at the other end was dead . . . no more sobs, nothing at all. Then, suddenly, a man's voice came on. "Hello . . . hello."

"Jinx! Jinx, is that you?" Alec thought it might be the hired man who took care of the farm's broodmares.

"Yes, this is Jinx. Is this really *you*, Alec?"

"Jinx, listen to me. I'm alive and in Preston, Arizona. Did you get that, Jinx?"

The voice at the other end descended to barely more than a whisper. "Yes, I heard you, Alec. I'll tell Henry and your father at once. They're in town. I was just passing by the house when your mother . . ." Jinx's voice trailed off.

"Ask Henry to come out here," Alec said. "He'll take this better than Dad."

"Yes, Alec."

When Alec hung up the phone, the door opened and two men rushed into the room. One said, "We're from the *Journal.* We had a call from the track from someone named Gordon who said *this kid is Alec Ramsay*!"

Allen and the Leesburg sheriff nodded their heads. "That might be his name, all right," Allen said. "At least he said so before. But what difference . . ."

The Preston police captain turned quickly to Allen and the Leesburg sheriff. "But you booked him as McGregor! If he should be *Alec Ramsay . . .*" He swept a startled look at the boy. *"Is* that your name?"

"Yes, that's my name. I've had amnesia."

For a moment the police captain just stared at Alec, and then his face turned red in anger. His eyes raked Allen. "Why didn't you tell me that when you brought him in here!"

Allen said sheepishly, "It's hard for me to think of him as anyone but McGregor."

"And the name Alec Ramsay meant nothing to you when he told you who he was?"

"No," Allen said. "Should it have?" He glanced worriedly toward the newspaper men, who were already taking pictures and making notes.

The police captain turned to the Leesburg sheriff. "And you, Tom? It meant nothing to *you*?"

"Now that you mention it, I think I might have heard something a couple of months ago about an Alec Ramsay . . ."

The police captain threw up his hands in disgust. "He's only been the subject of one of the biggest searches ever conducted in Wyoming,'' he shouted furiously.

One of the reporters spoke to Alec. ''That horse you rode today. Was he really *the Black* as we've been told by this man Gordon?''

''Yes,'' Alec said. ''Somehow he got here, too. I didn't know it was he until the race, when my memory came back.''

''You mean,'' the reporter said, ''that you didn't know who you were or what horse you were riding until the actual running of the race?''

Alec nodded. ''Not until almost the end of it,'' he said.

The reporter grabbed the phone. ''I got to get this to my editor,'' he told the police captain. ''This news is going to 'make' Preston like nothing ever did before. Once it goes out on the wires, we'll have a representative from every big paper in the country coming here!''

The police captain nodded. He turned to Allen and the Leesburg sheriff. ''And you two never even heard of Alec Ramsay and the Black,'' he said, shaking his head. Finally he turned to Alec. ''I guess you'd better stay here for the night. We can make you comfortable and afford you some protection from all the newsmen who'll be arriving before long. And, since we've already sent out your fingerprints to the Salt Lake City police, we'd better wait for an answer from them. That'll clear that incident up, and satisfy *him.*'' He nodded his head toward the Leesburg sheriff.

Alec turned to Allen. ''You didn't know, boss,'' he said. ''Believe me, I sure appreciate all you did for me. There are a lot of others who wouldn't have known, either. It isn't as bad as you're being led to believe.'' He paused, waiting for Allen to lift his gaze. "I wish you'd do me a favor. Go to the track and have Hank take the Black—or Range Boss, if you want to call him that—back to the ranch. It'll be better if he's kept away from all this."

"Sure, Mac. I'll do it right now." Allen hurried to the door, glad of an opportunity to escape the scathing remarks of the police captain.

The reporter had finished the telephone call to his editor, and was now bombarding Alec with questions. The boy answered quickly. He realized this was just the beginning, and that his call home hadn't been necessary at all in order for his parents and Henry to learn of his whereabouts. Within a few short hours the news of his being in Preston would be in every newspaper in the country. He hoped Henry would get here soon.

By late afternoon, newspaper correspondents from nearby cities had arrived. And by evening the number had grown considerably. They descended upon Preston's small courthouse, jamming the room. Alec sat in a chair answering all questions put to him, cooperating in every way he could by telling the reporters the complete story. The newsmen listened attentively to him, to Allen, to anyone who would give them something they could telephone to their papers. They learned of the match race, and soon the story of Night Wind's crushing defeat by the Black was released to the world.

All that night, the reporters and photographers stayed in Preston, knowing that before many hours Henry Dailey would arrive by plane. Alec slept on a cot, waiting too for Henry's arrival.

By morning, word was received from Salt Lake City

that Alec Ramsay's fingerprints were not those of the boy wanted by the police there. This information the police captain turned over to the Leesburg sheriff. "They must think we're fools down here," he said gruffly.

A plane from the East was due in Preston at seven o'clock, and the reporters, having learned that Henry was on it, went to the airport. A short while later they returned, and Henry strode belligerently into the court-room. Yet when Alec ran to meet him, Henry's stocky body slumped, and he wept unashamedly with his arms around the boy.

Finally he said, "Y-you're all right, Alec?"

"Sure, Henry. Mom and Dad? Are they . . ."

"They're okay now . . . they're waiting. You're cer-tain you're all right? The reporters in New York said . . ."

"I've had amnesia, but I'm fine now. I've felt pretty good all along, except that I couldn't remember any-thing."

"Have you seen a doctor?"

"No, it's not necessary. I'm all right, I tell you."

"You're going to see one. Here and in New York, too."

The photographers were taking pictures of them, and the reporters pushed close. Henry answered their ques-tions for a while, and then decided he'd had enough. "That's all," he said. "We're going now, and we don't want anyone following. Alec needs a rest, and you've got everything there is for your stories."

Outside, Henry had a taxi waiting. Alec glanced back and saw Allen standing silently among all the newsmen.

"Come on, boss," he called to him.

When they were the taxi he said, "This is Mr. Allen, Henry. I've been working for him. He raises quarter race horses."

Henry turned quickly to Allen. "You call yourself a horseman an' you didn't even recognize *him* all this time," he said angrily.

Allen's slight figure slumped in the corner of the seat. "I—I only follow q-quarter horse racing," he said.

Alec said, "Please, Henry. You're expecting too much from him. Of course he wouldn't know. He didn't have any way of knowing." Alec paused. "And without him, the Black and I might not have gotten together. I owe him an awful lot, Henry."

The trainer said softly, "I know, Alec. I'm sorry, Allen, and I apologize. It's just that it's been so long . . . and we'd given up all hope." He turned to look out the window of the moving taxi before adding, "And now I want to have a doctor see you, Alec. Maybe you know a good one here in town, Allen."

"Yes, I do," the rancher said, eager to be of help.

"After that," Henry added, "we'll go to Leesburg. I want to see the Black, and then we'll have to make arrangements to take him back with us."

"I wish you'd spend a few days as my guest," Allen said quickly.

"Thanks, but I know Alec is eager to get home, and his folks are just as eager to see him."

Alec thought of his mother and father waiting, and his eyes blurred. "I can phone them when we get to the ranch," he thought. "This time it'll be all right, I know."

Henry said, "We'll take the Black home by *train.*"

"We sure will," Alec said. "No planes for us, not for a while, anyway."

Toward evening of the same day, they arrived at the ranch. Alec and Henry went directly to the big corral. The Black saw them coming and, snorting, moved over to the bars. Alec put his hand on him. He noticed that the stallion's eyes were on Henry, never leaving him for a moment.

"I'm getting old," Henry said. "I don't trust my sight any more."

"It's the Black, all right, Henry," Alec said. He couldn't smile, couldn't make light of Henry's finding it so difficult to believe they were all together again.

"He's been cut up pretty bad."

"Yes, some scars, but he's fit, Henry."

"I know," the trainer agreed. "He never looked better. His good physical condition carried him through these last two months, the same as the doctor said about you. I guess you were both ready for the punishment you had to take."

Alec said nothing. The Black turned away from Henry to nuzzle the boy's hand. Alec stroked him for a few minutes, and then said, "He got more freedom than either of us bargained for, all right."

"Yeah, a lot more. Alec . . ."

"Yes, Henry?"

"It must have been a race to see, his whipping Night Wind like they say he did."

"It was a race to ride, I know that," Alec answered.

"He didn't have any trouble at all with Night Wind?"

"No, not once I stopped fighting him and gave him his head."

"He didn't make any attempt to attack Night Wind during the race?"

"No, Henry, not at all. Perhaps he got all the fighting out of his system while he was running wild. I don't know."

"Maybe you're right," Henry agreed. He watched the Black move away from Alec to go to the other side of the corral; there the stallion neighed to the group of mares in the adjacent corral. "Are those mares from his band?"

"Yes."

Henry said, "I suppose he'll miss 'em but we got plenty of mares back at the farm to interest him."

"Then you think it's absolutely safe to take him back home?"

"Sure. Don't you?" Henry asked.

"Yes, I guess so. It hasn't been the kind of a vacation we had planned for him, but he probably had a far better time of it."

"Yes, since he was lucky enough to stay alive," Henry returned quietly. He was thinking that it wasn't the vacation they had planned for Alec either, but said nothing more.

Hank Larom came out of the ranch house, and joined them beside the fence. Alec introduced them, and then Larom said, "Allen tells me you'll be leaving soon. I wish you could stay, Alec."

Henry put his arm around Alec. "We got his mother

and father waiting for him, Hank,'' he said, ''. . . and lots of other people.''

Larom nodded. ''I'll bet they're all anxious to see the Black again, too.'' He didn't take his eyes off the stallion. ''There'll never be another horse like him out here.''

''There just might be,'' Alec said quietly.

Larom turned, smiling. ''You goin' to bring him back some day, Alec?''

''I don't know about that, Hank. But didn't I hear Allen tell you, just before we left for Preston, that those mares from the Black's band were yours for the asking?''

''Yeah, he said that. I'll probably take them and sell 'em.''

''I'd take them and *keep* them, if I were you, Hank,'' Alec said. ''Chances are that some of them are in foal, and he's a pretty good sire.''

For a moment Larom was silent. Finally he said, ''I never gave that a thought, Alec. You sure could be right.'' He flicked a glance at the ranch house. ''When I left Allen a few minutes ago, he'd succeeded in getting hold of Herbert over at Preston. He wanted to make certain Herbert wasn't going to get out of giving him those quarter mares. Maybe this is a good time to remind Allen of the offer he made me.''

After Larom had left them, Alec called the Black, and the stallion came quickly to him.

Henry said, ''From what you've told me, Alec, I guess we could even race him on the big tracks without his gettin' into trouble. That is,'' he added hastily, ''if you wanted to race him.'' Henry looked hopefully at Alec.

"There'll be time enough later to talk about that," Alec said.

Larom and Allen came out of the ranch house. When they neared the corral, Larom winked at Alec, and the boy knew that Hank had been successful in getting the Black's mares *and* the foals to come.

Allen was grinning. "Just got through talking to Ralph Herbert on the phone," he said. "He's burned up because Range Boss won, but he's going to ship me his quarter mares by the first of next week. I'm all set now. By next year I'll have the best foals in the state."

"I'm not so sure of that," Hank Larom said, but only Alec heard him.

"Oh, *Mac,*" Allen went on, "that reminds me. The phone was ringing when I got back. It was Slim Gordon in Leesburg. He wanted me to tell you that he'll be reading some magazine called *Thoroughbred Record* regularly from now on, so he'll be keeping posted on how you and Range Boss are doing at the races back east."

Alec smiled. "Thanks, *boss.*" He rubbed the Black's neck. Maybe Slim Gordon would be reading about them. Maybe they'd be racing again. Maybe so.

ABOUT THE AUTHOR

Walter Farley's love for horses began when he was a small boy living in Syracuse, New York, and continued as he grew up in New York City, where his family moved. Unlike most city children, he was able to fulfill this love through an uncle who was a professional horseman. Young Walter spent much of his time with this uncle, learning about the different kinds of horse training and the people associated with each.

Walter Farley began to write his first book, *The Black Stallion,* while he was a student at Brooklyn's Erasmus Hall High School and Mercersburg Academy in Pennsylvania. He finished it and had it published while he was still an undergraduate at Columbia University.

The appearance of *The Black Stallion* brought such an enthusiastic response from young readers that Mr. Farley went on to write more stories about the Black, and about other horses as well. He now has twenty-five books to his credit, including his first dog story, *The Great Dane Thor,* and his story of America's greatest thoroughbred, *Man O' War.* His books have been enormously successful in this country, and have also been published in fourteen foreign countries.

When not traveling, Walter Farley and his wife, Rosemary, divide their time between a farm in Pennsylvania and a beach house in Florida.